SWEET TREATS

ICE CREAM

2022

ROMANCE
WRITERS
of Australia

Ice Cream 2022 Sweet Treats Anthology

Anthology of Short Stories published by Romance Writers of Australia

Inc © 2022

eBook format: 978-0-6452177-1-1

Print format: 978-0-6452177-2-8

Sweet Treats Coordinator: Paquita Fadden

Cover design by Kim Lambert – Dreamstone Publishing

Edited by Vikki Steele

Formatting by Kim Lambert

OTHER SWEET TREATS ANTHOLOGIES

Cupcake 2020

Chocolate 2021

SWEET TREATS

ICE CREAM

Short Story Anthology

2022

ALISON MIDDLETON	JACINTA PEACHEY
SUE-ELLEN PASHLEY	BRIDGET W DEEN
FIONA M MARSDEN	CHELSEA LOCKE
NICKI BURNS	CLARE MILES
VICTORIA BROWN	LUCY LEVER
CAROLINE DENESS	VALERIE G MILLER
KAAREN SUTCLIFFE	ANNETTE LEIGH
JILLIAN JONES	DENISE ASTON

CONTENTS

FOREWORD

Cold and creamy, with a multitude of flavours, who doesn't love an ice cream on a hot summers' day? Or even lashed with warm chocolate fudge in winter? In a sundae, with hot apple pie, or in a spider.

Sorry, time to stop drooling, and start enjoying these sixteen delectable short stories with frozen deliciousness.

Whatever you enjoy, you'll find a bit of everything in this collection.

We have so many talented authors that are part of the Romance Writers of Australia, and every year these anthologies just keep getting better, every year the choices just keep being harder. I am so proud of all the hard work that our members put in to these stories each and every year, and I just know you will enjoy everything you will find in these pages.

Grab yourself some frozen goodness now and prepare to enjoy our 2022 Sweet Treats Anthology – Ice Cream.

Tracey Rosen

President

Romance Writers of Australia

I

WHISKED AWAY

ALISON MIDDLETON

Chapter One

Love spells aren't like they are in the movies.

For Grace Henderson, the basics went well beyond bell, book and candle. She loved the ceremony and theatre of kitchen witchery and thought of her potions as a little drop of benevolence rippling through the pool of her local community.

Part of the fun was that she could add some healing elixirs to her array of ice creams and offer them up as samples to her favourite customers.

The teen worrying about exams loved the creamy lavender and rosemary infusion she'd whipped up to work wonders for both memory and anxiety. The sleep-deprived teacher relied on her passionflower sorbet. And the pensioner with arthritis had devoured the turmeric and ginger ice cream she'd churned by hand to aid inflammation.

Everyone in the village eventually found themselves in Whisked Away, often pulling up a chair or making a cup of tea as she bustled around in the cosy kitchen.

And if she meddled a little bit in people's love lives with the odd love spell to bring soulmates together, then who was going to argue?

Her wild strawberry, chocolate and chilli ice cream was a best seller and had brought dozens of couples together over the last few years.

Grace stirred the pot clockwise, adding a judicious hint of sea salt and three drops of the love potion she'd brewed the night before. The energy of the blue moon — the second full moon in a calendar month — was three times as powerful as a normal full moon, providing exactly the romantic kick that she was looking for. This little vial would go a long, *long* way.

The mixture was ready for churning and finished with just enough time to whip up some treats for the charity raffle before that night's council meeting.

Life would be close to perfect if not for a new police sergeant who'd breezed into their village from the city a few months ago. James Fitzwilliam had somehow managed to charm the *entire* population and had been insufferable ever since.

Her anger at Sergeant Fitzwilliam and his abrupt manner was almost enough to make her resort to the dark arts.

As it was, Grace had vividly imagined dropping her cauldron on his perfect boots, smacking him on the head with a besom or cursing him to a lifetime of premature ejaculation.

She'd contented herself with small curses: socks slipping down in his shoes, traffic lights at red when he was running late and continually running out of loo paper at the most inconvenient time possible.

Small stuff.

If it seemed like her feelings for the man bordered on the irrational, then clearly it was just her witchy powers which enabled her to see through his bullshit.

Grace let energy flow through her as she mixed up the batch of chocolate brownies in record time under the watchful eye of Elphaba, her black rescue cat.

Flour, chocolate, sugar, eggs and vanilla extract were all coming together perfectly — with a secret ingredient or two — to make the treats irresistible.

Closing her eyes, Grace muttered her spell and wished for the raffle winner to find their heart's true desire. Her eyes were still closed when Elphaba's delicate paw reached out to knock the little bottle over, sending the rest of the love potion into the mixture.

Unaware of the unexpected addition, Grace beamed as she gave the mixture a final stir, poured the chocolate sludge into a tray and pushed it into the oven. The empty vial spun clockwise, unnoticed on the shelf.

CRED   CRED

Chapter Two

Grace took her seat at the council meeting and dipped into her bag to pull out a tub stuffed with chocolate brownies. She briefly caught James's eye and gave him a bright smile designed to irritate as she visualised smacking him over the head with his own baton.

"Grace." He nodded.

Full stop. She could bloody well hear the full stop after her name.

Grace felt her hackles rise high enough to scrape the ceiling and stuck her tongue out behind his back as he walked away. Of course, she didn't bank on him turning around and catching her in the act.

He rolled his eyes in response, shaking his head as he rolled up his sleeves.

"Oh, hey Mrs Elder," Grace said to an older woman sitting down beside her.

"You're still fighting with the handsome new sergeant then," the woman laughed, raising an eyebrow. "Energy flows where attention goes — and that man has been getting an awful lot of your attention lately."

Grace tutted. "We don't get on. That's all. You can't expect to like everyone. Even in a nice place like this."

Could the old woman's eyebrow get any higher? Apparently so.

"My dear, it would appear that you protest too much. And he certainly isn't short of appeal. Where else in this town are you going to find a nice man who looks like *that* with *those* forearms?"

Grace raised an eyebrow of her own.

"I hadn't noticed. And even if he is tall and not completely heinous looking, he's rude and arrogant."

Mrs Elder's eyes narrowed as she pulled out a thermos of hot chocolate and passed a cup to Grace.

Grace made the best ice cream and desserts in the village, but no-one could hold a candle (bewitched or otherwise) to Mrs Elder's hot chocolate.

"Is he? Are you sure about that? Not everyone brags about their good deeds, my dear. And not everyone is blessed with such a happy manner as you. Did you ever think that maybe he's just shy?"

With that, the meeting started. But Grace's attention wasn't on the debate about recycling bins or plans for a new school playing field. No, her eyes were on the man in blue sitting in the front row.

Maybe he could feel her gaze, because at the end of the meeting, when he stood up, his eyes met hers. It only took a moment, but the feeling was a lot like being drawn towards a magnet and hit with a tuning fork at the same time. At least until he looked away awkwardly. He'd left immediately afterwards.

Despite that weird moment, it had been a good day, Grace mused later that night. The sergeant had won the raffle and the village was another step closer to a cohesive recycling plan. And then there was that strange chat with Mrs Elder.

She was just climbing into bed with her favourite Jane Austen novel and a cup of spearmint and lavender tea when the phone rang.

"Grace, it's James. Sergeant James Fitzwilliam," he added when she didn't immediately respond.

"Um. Hello." Grace cleared her throat. "Can I help you?"

"I'm sorry to call so late, but Mrs Elder has had a fall. She gave your details as her emergency contact. She's ok — no serious injury — but she's at the community hospital and she's asking for you."

Grace was already leaping out of bed and pulling a thick fisherman's knit jumper over her pyjamas.

"I'll be right there."

ೞ൜ഏ   ೞ൜ഏ

Chapter Three

The next day Grace arrived at Mrs Elder's house, cradling a basket full of vegetable soup, some homemade bread and yet more of her ubiquitous ice cream.

Mrs Elder would be getting out of hospital later that day, after being kept in overnight for observation.

She'd escaped with only bumps and bruises, but Grace didn't want her coming back to a cold house. A hot meal and a good fire would help settle her at home and reassure her after the shock of the fall.

She was surprised to find the door already unlocked with a fire crackling merrily in the grate and a newly chopped stack of firewood ready and waiting.

A pot of something delicious simmered on the stove, the floor looked freshly swept and a bouquet of local wildflowers was taking centre stage in the country farmhouse-style kitchen.

"Have Snow White's woodland animals been here? Can you send them round to mine afterwards?" Grace called.

The sound of heavy boots coming through from the back door drew her attention, and James emerged carrying an armful of firewood.

"Grace."

There was that full stop again, but it didn't bother her as much as it had before.

"James."

He'd been so good last night, waiting with her to see Mrs Elder and then making sure she got home safely to the little flat above Whisked Away. He'd even walked her to her door.

"No woodland animals, I'm afraid. Unless you count the ones in the stew. Sorry, nervous humour..."

He tailed off, running a large, calloused hand through his dark hair.

"This is amazing. Did you do all of this?"

"Great minds think alike." He gestured to her heavily laden arms and pulled the ice cream from her basket to stash in the freezer. "What kind of ice cream did you make her this time?"

"Chamomile and honey to help with healing and shock. It's pretty tasty, too." She couldn't help but smile as she looked at him.

"I do love how much thought you put into your ice creams. You seem to know what everyone needs."

"Not everyone..." she whispered. "You're hard to read. And I think I may have misjudged you. I'm sorry for that. Thank you for everything you've done for Mrs Elder."

He gave her a shy smile. Goddess, have mercy. The man had dimples.

"That's ok. I know I come off as abrupt sometimes. I'm sorry for not being friendlier. It takes time for me to get to know people, that's all."

Chapter Four

Over the next few weeks, Grace felt she and James had fallen into a rhythm.

Push, pull. Circle. Closer.

Sergeant James Fitzwilliam had even inspired a new ice cream flavour.

The ice cream was an apt metaphor for whatever was growing between them. After she'd stopped seeing him as the devil (and stopped her passive aggressive hexes), they'd found their way to a clean slate, much like her vanilla ice cream.

She'd stirred a bay leaf infusion with crushed peppercorns mingling with the seeds of the vanilla to create an ice cream which combined purity and spice in an addictive combination that she could definitely get used to.

Grace had thought of him and his small acts of kindness as she ground the herbs together in a pestle and mortar. Remembered how kind he'd been in checking up on Mrs Elder as she whisked the cream. How his green eyes sparkled when someone made him laugh. How badly she'd wanted to touch him for comfort at the hospital. And then for a very different reason when she couldn't sleep.

She'd eventually dozed off wondering what his stubble would feel like against her cheek, her lips, her tongue. And other places. She'd thought of him as she'd stirred the concoction and blessed it to keep him safe.

Grace blushed. The mixture definitely had a kick to it and let's just say that she'd started to notice that Mrs Elder hadn't been wrong about his forearms. How had she ever thought that the man was cold? He was like an impressionist painting —

every time she saw him, she noticed something she'd never seen before, and the overall picture became even more beautiful as a result.

The moon was once again full and round in the sky as Grace hurried to Mrs Elder's home for their weekly dinner date with James.

They'd discovered that while she excelled at desserts, James's culinary skillset tended towards the savoury, and he was sure to have brought around something for Sunday dinner.

Sure enough, he was there, pulling a lasagne out of the oven as she blustered into the kitchen and shut the door against the wind.

He'd poured her a glass of red wine before she'd even taken off her coat. Now the weather was getting colder she'd brought out her winter repertoire — chocolate mousses, baked Alaska and sticky toffee puddings.

While they'd fallen into the habit of meeting at Mrs Elder's for dinner every week, it was probably no coincidence that she tried to outdo herself trying to find his favourite pudding.

Looking into his eyes, Grace shivered despite the warmth of the fire as the energy shifted in the room.

There was a long pause before their fingertips met on the rough surface of the kitchen table. No sound except an odd emphatic spark from the fire and the rustle of the wind outside.

Their fingers interlaced as they held eye contact for what felt like hours. Grace tried to speak. Tried to say what she was feeling, but the words scattered as his thumb gently traced the sensitive skin of her palm.

She wasn't sure who moved first. Only that she was in his arms and his mouth was on hers, her knees buckling under the sheer sensation.

His arms tightened around her, and she knew he'd never let her fall.

When they eventually pulled away from the kiss, his forehead leaned against hers and she could feel his heartbeat pounding.

"I've wanted to do that since the day we met. Even though you looked like you wanted to throw a tub of ice cream at my head.

"Also, side note. At some point we need to talk about your brownies. They're too good. Seriously, I've been eating one a day for the past month."

"One a day?" Grace gulped. "So basically, since the last full moon. Well, *fuck*."

"What?" James looked confused. "Aren't you supposed to be happy that I liked your baking?"

"But I put a love spell in those brownies, and that was before the rest of my most powerful love potion somehow managed to get tipped into the batch! In witchy layman's terms, you got hit with a super dose that was enough for dozens of people. If you stay — if you say that you have feelings for me — I won't know if it's because of the spell."

Grace's breath was uneven as she tried to push down the wave of sheer panic, also known as *feelings*, and gulped for air.

"Grace. Breathe," James said softly, cradling her face in his hands.

"I was crazy about you long before I ate all the brownies. This isn't a new feeling — for either of us. It's just new talking about it."

"Well, it's about bloody time," Mrs Elder cackled from the landing.

"You shouldn't be on your feet," Grace shouted back.

"My dear, I'm as fit as a fiddle. Did you think you were the only witch in the village? Or the only one capable of meddling? It was about time someone gave you a taste of your own medicine, so to speak. Even if had to stage a little accident to get you both to finally admit that you're mad for each other."

"You conniving, meddlesome..." Grace tailed off. "Just for that I'm putting eye of newt into your next batch of ice cream!"

"Takes one to know one," Mrs Elder sang. "You've been so afraid of your feelings for that man that you've been low-key cursing him for months just so you can keep your walls up. No wonder he was too scared to ask you out!

"You made it easy for me — I even used your own love spell! Whisked Away indeed, my dear. Kudos by the way, that worked a treat. And especially well in hot chocolate."

James shook his head.

"You staged an accident so you could play matchmaker? You do realise that I could charge you for wasting police time? But since I have the woman of my dreams in my arms, I think I'll settle for you cooking for *us* next Sunday. And pretty much every Sunday for the rest of the year."

"Happy to, my dear. You and Grace can bring dessert."

And with that final word, Mrs Elder sauntered off, very much looking like the cat with the cream.

"Well, she's certainly creative," James mused as Grace stared after the old woman.

"Speaking of creativity... You know, I hate to say it, but I think I've come up with a way to improve one of your ice creams." James looked thoughtful.

"Hear me out. Chocolate brownies *in the ice cream.* It's the way forward. I'm a genius. You're welcome. Don't believe me? We should go try that right now."

"You just want to lick the spoon," Grace teased, staring into his darkened eyes that were looking at her with wonder and more than a hint of mischief.

"Baby, you have no idea. Let's go — you've already bewitched me, now it's your turn to get whisked away."

2

THE FLATMATE

JACINTA PEACHEY

What a day! Gracie slumped on the couch eating ice cream straight from the tub. Her go-to food for miserable moods. So many things had happened in twenty-four hours and ice cream was healthier than drinking into oblivion. You don't drunk-text ex-boyfriends or give your mother a piece of your mind when you're high on sugar and your stomach's churning from excess dairy. Yep, much safer than tequila. When everything in life sucks, you can count on ice cream.

A large spoonful of chocolate chip melted on her tongue, its cool creaminess a salve for a troubled mind. Three scented candles and a depressing playlist turned up loud helped block all thoughts of the day's troubling events.

A key jiggled in the lock — her flatmate Will was home.

Gorgeous unavailable Will.

"Oh no." Will dropped his keys in the bowl on the hall table. "What's happened?"

"What do you mean?"

Trying to sit up, she slipped deeper, stuck between two seat cushions. The couch, taken from a roadside collection, had questionable springs, and if you got into the wrong spot, it sucked you into the black hole where socks and Tupperware lids went to die.

"You're wearing fifteen-year-old track pants and your high school t-shirt." Will turned down the sound and sniffed. "The music is wailing and you're eating out of the tub. I doubt you've had a post-work shower either."

She waved her spoon, dismissing the comment. At least he didn't mention the messy hair or streaky make-up after hours of crying.

Will removed his satchel and sat opposite Gracie on the 1990s hardwood coffee table they'd found in a garage sale. For the last month, he had worked as a nurse doing night shifts at the local hospital, while Gracie did days. Rarely seeing each other, they had communicated via cheeky Post-it notes and silly text messages.

"Do you want to talk?" He gently prised the spoon out of her hand. "I'll listen if you'll share your ice cream."

His warm brown eyes were her undoing. The kindness that glimmered in his gaze was the reason his patients loved him. She tipped the tub toward him, not letting go, knowing his tactic was to take it to stop her eating and get her talking.

"It's my favourite." Will arched his eyebrows. "How many back-up tubs in the freezer?" He heaped the spoon.

"Two. Café Grande and chocolate. They were out of Cookies and Cream."

"A three-tub drama. Not good." He tried to wrestle the tub away but failed. "What's happened?"

"What hasn't happened? Mum and Kev are flying to New Zealand next weekend to elope and I can't get time off."

Kevin had made her mother so happy over the last five years that Gracie craved a similar relationship. Singledom was overrated. She pulled out a second spoon tucked in her pocket — a good nurse is always prepared.

"The short notice sucks," Will said. "At least you don't have to wear the pink taffeta dress."

He grinned and took another scoop. Typical Will, trying to make her smile in a crisis. Her mother had a bridesmaid's dress from her first wedding that she threatened to make Gracie wear if she ever married for a fourth time. Drop-waisted with puffy sleeves wasn't anyone's style.

"What's really the problem? I know that's not it. You've hoped they'd get married for ages."

Gracie wanted to attend the wedding, but after a long conversation with her mum, she understood. Kevin's mother, at ninety-two, was ill, and too old and frail to fly. Her last request was to see him married.

"I'm thrilled for them and I wish I could be there. They're the perfect couple." She took a scoop, focusing on a drip building on the edge of the spoon. "No-one wants me."

"Rubbish. You've got loads of friends. Me included." He shook his head, then motioned for the tub. "Your pity-party is a bit pathetic."

He watched her, waiting. With quieter background music, the lack of noise made her squirm, slipping further into the couch.

"I haven't received a notification from my dating app in days." The lack of contact had added to the day's feelings of loneliness. The dates were usually dismal, but it gave her a reason to get out and try to find someone special.

"Is that because you changed your photo to a potato and updated your profile to a list of basic facts?"

"Oh no, my drunken tirade last Saturday." She wiggled out of the gap and positioned herself securely on a cushion further away from Will. "It's all coming back to me."

She had stood on the table and ranted that men should love her regardless of prettiness or how wittily she could describe herself in 100 words. She opened the app to reveal the evidence.

"I also added a 500-metre limited search radius. My mobile needs an alcohol detector that disables access at readings over 0.08."

Will grabbed the tub.

"At least today you're gorging on ice cream and won't do anything silly."

Last Saturday's date was punctual and cute. Within five minutes, he had started talking about his ex-girlfriend, which wasn't a first for Gracie. But when he wanted a photo of them together to prove to his mother he was over the ex, Gracie raced to join her friends who were drinking nearby to workshop everything.

When she finally got home drunk late on Saturday, Will and his girlfriend Elise were still up chatting. Gracie ranted, and Will listened, offering advice. Elise stormed off to Will's bedroom, probably because they had left her out of the conversation again. He followed to smooth over the issue and Gracie headed to bed, drowning out the sounds of their fight with music.

"There's someone out there for you," he said.

"Yeah, yeah, expect it when you least expect it. Blah, blah. I don't need stupid platitudes, thanks. I've heard them all."

"Ahh, we are reaching the 'woe is me phase' as you near the end of the first litre. You know what goes well with ice cream?"

He waved the almost empty tub.

"Dessert wine?" Gracie snatched it back and scraped up the dregs.

"No," Will said.

"Champagne? Pink gin?"

"Proper food or a walk. You'll thank me tomorrow when your stomach isn't hurting and you haven't gained three kilos."

She poked out her tongue, not caring if it was covered in milky residue.

"Food schmood."

"Have a shower Gracie, you'll feel better." Will stood, taking her spoon and the empty tub.

Ice cream wouldn't numb the pain of the day. It was more than the lack of interest in her dating app. "Beth died last night."

"I'm sorry." He reached out and touched her shoulder. The casual contact sent shivers down her arm. "She was your favourite, wasn't she?"

"Yep." She choked on a sob. Gracie had nursed Beth for the last few weeks. Beth's GP had fobbed off her abdominal pain as just women's issues, telling her extra tests were unnecessary. When she was finally admitted to hospital with vomiting, severe cramps and constipation, they detected a bowel blockage from extensive intestinal cancer. Palliative care was the only option. Forty-eight was too young to die.

Will sat next to Gracie on the couch and gathered her weeping defenceless body into his arms. "That sucks."

She cried into his shoulder, enjoying the familiarity of his body. It wasn't the first time they had sobbed over a patient. They supported each other through the bad and celebrated the good.

The warmth of his arms as her tears subsided sent her heart thumping. None of her dates ever created the same effect as Will.

He drew back and looked her in the eye.

"Time for a shower. I'll order our healthy takeout option."

"Thai beef salad and stir-fry veg," they said in unison.

"Can we get a serve of extra spicy larb too? That comes with lettuce, so technically a vegetable and healthy." She smiled. Humour was necessary to stem the tears.

"Not a lot of fibre, but you can have larb. Now shower. You've got that irresistible scent of too much dairy, hand sanitiser with a dab of hospital-grade disinfectant and four-day-old hair."

She choked on a laugh, but stomped to the bathroom hoping twenty minutes of running water could wash away the grief.

ᏮᏗᏠᏯ

The candles were gone, the music was more upbeat but not too loud and the spicy smell of Thai wiped away the pity-party of thirty minutes ago. A long shower and a pair of snuggly pink flannel pyjamas had Gracie feeling half-decent. It wouldn't solve the biggest issue, but she had compartmentalised the grief. As an oncology nurse, she'd learnt early on how to cope with loss. Knowing she had provided comfort to patients in their last days was rewarding.

Seated side-by-side with Will, the takeaway containers on the coffee table, as usual, Gracie dished up stir-fry, removing the carrots from Will's plate, and giving him extra capsicum, while he poured glasses of wine.

"I can't believe the hospital's doing another cost-cutting drive." She stabbed a fork in the air, still skirting the actual issue. "No more biscuits in the staff room. It's apparently good for our health and the budget."

"After excess ice cream, you'll be glad of no temptations at work." Will carefully filled a lettuce leaf with the spicy larb, his long fingers precisely layering the chicken with extra chillies.

"You're not cheering me up."

"Budget cuts suck." Will winked. "I loathe sugar-haters."

They laughed. Will could always make her smile. Living with him for the last two years was both wonderful and detrimental. She compared her dates to him and no-one lived up to the feelings she harboured. The only way to find someone special was to get away.

"I've got more bad news. The lease is due and the rent's increasing by ten percent."

"Have you got anything good to say?" he asked.

"Sorry, I'm Donna Doomy today. I don't know why you put up with me except I pay half the rent." She tried for a smile and Will frowned. He probably thought she was fishing for compliments. "Today's got me thinking. I need to live a fuller life because who knows when your number's up."

"Not exactly cheery, but positive. What are you planning: skydiving or swimming with the sharks?"

"I might travel or get married before it's too late." She toyed with a piece of tomato, but it kept falling off her fork as her fingers shook. "My mother was on her second husband at my age."

"Are you looking for Mr Right on the dodgy app or somewhere new?"

She squashed the food. Who was he to mock her?

The dating world was tough enough without smug couples questioning your actions.

As they ate, the silence yawned, with only the clunk of cutlery on plates and the sound of Will chewing audible over the low music. To sign the lease for another six months was foolish. She couldn't continue sharing with a man she desired.

Besides, Will's relationship would improve when she left. He always got distracted when Gracie was around, and it made Elise angry. Even though she didn't think Elise was his perfect match, a good friend honoured others' love choices.

The first step of the change was finding new accommodation. Her mother had suggested buying something; a daring step at twenty-five. A little apartment or townhouse in the next suburb wasn't out of reach. Nothing big, two bedrooms. A fresh start. The money saved on missing the wedding would go towards the deposit, and her mum had promised to help.

"It's time I moved out rather than renew the lease. It's part of my forge a fresh path."

"What?" Will dropped his fork and rice splattered across the carpet. "Bugger."

She picked up the pieces of rice, putting them into a serviette. "You and Elise can move in together. After eighteen months, it's time." Gracie didn't need to see his look when he realised the opportunity her departure offered. She'd miss him. The ease of hanging out. How he finished her sentences and always said the right thing. They'd stay friends, but not seeing each other constantly would help them both.

"We broke up on the weekend," he muttered.

"What?" Gracie dropped the serviette, scattering rice across the floor. "I'm sorry. Why did you let me bleat on about my trashy day? I'd have dragged myself up from the Donna Doomy act and been a better friend."

He shrugged and splayed his hands, but didn't speak. It was worse than she imagined.

"Is that why I haven't seen you for days? The next tub of ice cream's all yours."

"I wasn't that upset. We had a row while you were on your date and when you got home, I chatted to you, making it worse. She stormed out in the early hours."

"But you were the perfect couple. You'll kiss and make up?" She nudged his shoulder encouragingly, feigning support.

"She gave me an ultimatum, and I didn't make the preferred choice." He pushed a piece of onion around his plate.

"Ultimatums are disastrous. My dating code is never make them unless you can live with the consequences. What did you choose?"

"You."

His word hung in the air as Gracie tried to decipher the intent, because his face gave nothing away.

"She made you choose between herself and your flatmate? Is she nuts?"

He shrugged, then cleaned up the mess on the floor.

"Aren't you upset?"

"Nah, Elise's right."

"Right about what?" Gracie and Elise never agreed, and she doubted Elise was correct about Will.

"I put you first all the time, and she hated it."

"But we're not a couple." Gracie topped up the wineglasses, thinking it was getting close to ice cream time. They had drunk enough. "Just good mates. Like brother and sister." Except her feelings for Will were far from brotherly.

Will didn't speak, and Gracie had to fill the void.

"I'm sorry. It's my fault. If I hadn't come home whinging about my date, this wouldn't have happened."

"We were fighting when you arrived. Your awful date was light relief. The fact he asked your shoe size was hilarious, but everything after that was next level." Will pushed his plate away and his fingers traced the edge of the table.

"Another dreadful night of my dating apps."

"It got to her that you and I are so in sync," he said. "More than Elise and I ever were. Lately I've been going through the motions without any emotion. If she hadn't broken up with me, I'd have done it once I worked out how to, without hurting her."

"Sometimes you can't avoid the pain. Best to do it like removing a surgical drain. Smooth but fast and continuous."

"Her yelling was continuous." He stretched his lips tight, but not into a smile. "She'd never have got that joke and hated me talking about work because it made her queasy. Long term, we were doomed to fail."

"You know, dating in the medical scene's difficult."

"It doesn't have to be when you find the right person."

"I've dated the lot. Doctors, nurses, orderlies, even a dentist. Let me tell you, having someone floss your teeth after eating steak is not sexy. It's a tough world out there."

"I think I may have found my perfect match." He smiled, and her heart thumped. Of course, a great guy like Will would get snapped up. Was it the new physio on his floor?

Gracie sipped her drink to wash away the rising acid as her guts clenched. Ice cream, stir-fry and white wine weren't a brilliant mix. Her mum was right. She needed to move on. Will was holding her back and she wouldn't get on with his next girlfriend, either.

"Lucky you. No need for dating apps. I'm jealous you found someone so quickly. I've been trying for years."

"Maybe you've been looking in the wrong places."

Gracie slammed her glass on the table. "I banned lousy dating cliches earlier. One more and you're on washing up for a week."

"Just like removing a surgical drain." He ran his hand through his hair. "Except I've failed at doing it smoothly, so will go for fast and continuous. I was hoping *you* might be interested in dating me. We're friends. We laugh at the same things. Like the same movies and foods, give or take ice cream flavours. Would you at least consider me?"

Her fingers clenched, and she exhaled slowly. Will wanted to date her.

"Sorry. Forget it," he muttered. "I know I'm not trendy or flashy like the guys you prefer. I'm just Will."

Just perfect Will. "Still not smooth, but your words are fast and continuous. I've got one cure for verbal diarrhoea." She leant forward. "I've wanted to do this for a long time."

They were close. His gaze focused on her lips as she licked them. Her mouth was dry as her courage deserted her despite the brazen words. Could she kiss Will?

His mouth was on her as her stagnant brain whirled. Soft spicy lips, slowly testing then an inquisitive slip of his tongue. Everything she wanted, and it sent shivers down her spine. Her shaking hands raked up his arms and his skin goose-pimpled. The effect she had on him embolden her. This was the man of her dreams, and it felt right.

Best kisses ever. Better than a bowl of Cookies and Cream. Better than going to her mother's wedding. He was a future she'd never dared to dream.

With Will by her side, she'd never gorge on tubs of ice cream again. From here on in, only two scoops, plus nuts and fudge sauce and maybe a swirl of caramel, sprinkled with a few shards of chocolate. She was in love, but not crazy.

3
ADVENTURE-SEEKING GODDESS

SUE-ELLEN PASHLEY

Week 1

"How can an empty wardrobe feel so devastating and yet, be such a relief at the same time?"

Sam, best friend, sympathiser and bringer of ice-cream, waved her spoon in the air.

"It's because you were ready for it to end even if you didn't want to acknowledge it. You and Simon haven't been good for a while. You know this."

I sighed. "I know. I *know*. But it seems so final. Five years of my life just... pfft. Like it never existed. I wanted to marry him."

Sam snorted and I frowned at her.

"What? I did!"

"No, you didn't," she said with what felt like an insulting level of assuredness. "You thought you *should* marry him, since you'd been together so long, but you didn't really want to."

I paused, spoon half buried in the ice-cream she'd brought, and looked out over my view of the park — the whole reason I'd bought the unit despite its seventies-entrenched brown and olive interior. The home Simon and I were going to make together; although, apparently, that had only been my dream. His dream, so he informed me as he left my life, was to travel to Alaska and become a world-famous environmental photographer.

It'd come as a bit of a shock really, given I'd had no idea he was into photography *or* the environment. I'd wanted to point out that I'd always been the one to take the recycling out, for God's sake, but it hadn't been worth the breath. He just would've given me that slightly sardonic look I'd grown to really hate in the last six months — the one that said he understood the world in a way he felt was beyond me.

"We're rooted in routine," he'd said. "I love you, Emma, but I need more. I need adventure and spontaneity. And I need to find it on my own."

"But you're an accountant! You love routine."

He'd touched my arm and I'd stepped back, out of his reach.

"I know this is hard and probably a bit unexpected but I need more and I think you do too. Are you happy — really?"

"Yes!" I'd said at the time but now, with Sam's words echoing in my brain, I wondered if I truly had been. Life with Simon had been... comfortable.

Predictable.

Stable.

Shit — he'd been right. We'd been rooted in routine; rotting in routine, really. And, if I was being honest, our love had been a part of that repetitiveness — something we did because we always had.

I sighed. "You're right."

"I know," she said, raising one eyebrow and licking the ice-cream from her spoon. "So, what now? It's been three months, Em. Time to shake it off. Unleash the divine, adventure-seeking Goddess I know is lurking inside you."

"Adventure-seeking Goddess?" I laughed. "I don't think I've ever been that."

"Well, it's time then. You're twenty-eight, not eighty-eight. And you don't need to have your whole life planned out." She pointed her finger at me. "Definitely compensating for the fact that you were always more of an adult that your mum ever was."

I rolled my eyes at her pop-psychology and finished scooping out some of the best-friend-in-crisis ice-cream she'd delivered. Even if there was some truth to what she was saying, I'd never admit it.

Had I been so busy being the responsible one all the time though, that I'd forgotten to have fun?

I absently put the spoon in my mouth, still thinking of Simon's words, and stopped, statue-still, as the flavours melted on my tongue.

"Sweet Jesus." I pulled the tub closer to me. "What is this, apart from orgasm on a spoon?"

Sam put another spoonful in her mouth before answering me, closing her eyes for a moment. "I know, right? *Pina Colada* — my favourite so far. The fact I'm sharing this with you is testament to how much I love you. I found them last week — *Sweet Pleasures*. It's made locally."

I filled my spoon again and let the deliciousness overwhelm my taste buds. Maybe it was the sugar hit or perhaps the hard-truth reflection, but it was time, I decided. Time for change.

I looked at Sam. "I need your help."

"Sure. What with?"

"I'm going to try to do something new, every week. Something I've never done before. But I need you to keep me honest — make sure I do it."

She grinned at me. "Deal. And your reward each week shall be a new flavour of *Sweet Pleasures*." She held up her spoon and I crossed my handle with hers to complete our pact. "You're going to make an awesome adventure-seeking Goddess."

∞∞   ∞∞

Week 2

It was impossible to sit on the grass without groaning on the way down. I had no idea how I was going to get back up but I needed to be in the park, surrounded by nature.

"Are you okay?"

The rich, masculine voice came from behind me and I spun as quickly as I could, which honestly wasn't that fast, to find the owner. He was perched in the low fork of a tree, book in hand, one leg swinging lazily, and warm coffee-coloured eyes looking at me with interest.

"Sorry?"

He smiled and a small part of me melted like chocolate in the sun.

"That sounded painful," he said, closing the book on his index finger. "I was just wondering if you were okay?"

My cheeks burned and I laughed. "Yes. First week of Hula Fit. I wasn't expecting it to be quite as hard on my body."

"Hula Fit?"

"Exercise with a hula hoop."

"Ah." There was something in the silence after this easy acceptance that made me want to keep talking — not to fill the space but because it felt... comfortable. Helped by the fact maybe that he was a stranger.

"This week was my test run. I don't think I'll be heading back."

"You like to try new things?"

I leant back, legs out in front of me. "Not usually but I've decided it's time for new adventures."

He acknowledged that with a nod and slipped down out of the tree, sinking athletically to the ground without groaning — show-off! — before leaning back against the tree trunk. Objectively, he was gorgeous. Dark hair that just called for fingers to be run through it, a dimple in his left cheek and a white buttoned-up shirt with rolled-up sleeves that showed off wide shoulders and toned arms. But somehow, the fact he was holding a book made him even more attractive.

"And is this your first new adventure?"

I realised, with blush-inducing mortification, that I'd been ogling his chest and had no idea what he'd asked. "Um, yes?"

He cocked his head. "So, this is your first adventure?"

"Oh," I said, brain rushing to keep up. "Yes, this was my first. I mean, not my first, obviously, because I've tried new things before but it's my first this time. An adventure virgin, if you like." Oh my god, why had I said that! Especially when it made no sense! Shit. Stop, Emma. But the words kept babbling out. "It was my friend's idea — Sam. She's buying me ice-cream each week as an incentive. *Sweet Pleasures*. That's what the ice-cream's called, I mean, not what..."

Finally, the words petered out.

He chuckled. Holy God, even his chuckle did things to my insides. "Yes, I've heard of the brand — my sister's a fan. Have you got a favourite flavour?"

"I've only had one — *Pina Colada*. Heaven on a spoon. We're trying another one tonight."

"Heaven on a spoon? I'll have to try it." He smiled at me and the heat intensified on my skin. I hadn't blushed this much since high school. "Have you decided on your next adventure?"

I licked my lips, mouth suddenly dry, and took a deep breath. "Roller derby." I couldn't believe I was telling him this, not when I wasn't sure yet that I was actually brave enough to follow through.

He lips quirked in a way that made it hard to look away. "Wow, that's adventurous. Can you skate?"

"Sure." I leant forward again, dusting off my hands, trying to look unconcerned at the fact I hadn't skated for fifteen years. It couldn't be that hard, surely — like riding a bike. "It's just trials so shouldn't be as full on as a game. And it's something I've never tried."

"Can I recommend the *Chocolate Jewel* ice-cream then, as your reward for being so adventurous? It's brownie, raspberry swirl — my sister's favourite."

"Sounds delicious." I sighed and looked around at the fading light. "Well, I suppose I need to find a way to get up and head home."

He stood, holding out his hand. "Allow me to be of assistance."

I wondered later if it was weird that I hadn't even hesitated. My hand felt small in his and when he pulled me up, I was close enough to see the gold flecks in his eyes. It made me strangely breathless — a flurry of warmth and promise. And when, after a few beats, our hands dropped apart, disappointment flooded through me.

"I'm Ben, by the way." He hadn't moved back and neither had I.

"Emma."

"Emma," he said, as if my name tasted good in his mouth. "Enjoy your *Sweet Pleasures*."

CRBO   CRBO

Week 3

Ben was reading in the tree again. I'd told myself I just wanted to walk in the park but honestly, I was hoping he'd be there. I'd been thinking about him all week — his eyes, his hands, the way he'd said my name...

As if he was waiting for me too, or maybe I was totally deluding myself, he closed his book as soon as he saw me and smiled.

"How did you survive roller derby?"

He winced as I showed him the bruises on my leg. "Ouch. And are you going back?"

I shook my head. "Definitely not. You should see the rest of my body — it's covered in bruises." And then I realised what I'd said and could feel the heat on my chest, burning its way up my neck, my face.

His mouth quirked. "I'm not averse to the idea if you wanted to show me."

My heart loudly signalled its agreement in morse code and I put my hand to my chest, trying to calm it.

"What flavour ice-cream did you get?"

I swallowed past the tightness in my throat. "*Mediterranean Bliss* — honey pistachio."

He nodded. "Interesting combination. What did you think?"

I walked closer, leaning against the branch he was sitting on. Under the canopy of rich, green leaves, it felt like our own little world.

"Amazing. But *Pina Colada* is still my favourite."

"A woman who's sure of what she enjoys. I like that."

Every organ in my body clenched at the look in his eyes, the tone of his voice and I had to deliberately stop myself taking a step closer to him — pulled like metal to a magnet.

"Do you always sit in a tree to read?"

He laughed, but ran his hand self-consciously through his hair. "Not always. But there's something... comforting about it. I used to do it as a kid and decided I needed to start again."

I tilted my head. "Why?"

"There's been a lot of change in my life the last six months, including starting a new business. I needed to go back to some of the things I knew I enjoyed — things that brought me pleasure. So, reading in a tree was one of them."

I liked that — the synchronicity of where we both were.

"And how are you going with the changes?"

A small smile graced his lips — there and gone — like a portent to a mystery I'd be happy to get to the bottom of. "Getting easier all the time. What do you do when you're not having new adventures?"

"Interior design."

"Do you enjoy it?"

I hesitated for a moment and then decided to tell the truth. It seemed easy to do that with him. "Yes, mostly. Although it's been recently pointed out to me that I have both a wide responsibility streak and a planning fixation, which probably makes me good at my job but doesn't work so well in other areas of my life. Hence, the need to explore becoming an adventure-seeking Goddess."

He chuckled, leaning forward along the branch, closer to me. "An adventure-seeking Goddess. That suits you."

A lightness filled my soul, which was ridiculous. He knew nothing about me. And yet, it was nice to be thought of as something more than the responsible one. Even Simon had seen me as that — always happy for me to fulfil that role even though that's what seemed to have driven him away in the end.

"I'm trying," I said and it felt, in that moment, like I might be able to get there.

"What's on the agenda for this week's adventure?"

I frowned. "I'm not sure. Honestly, something that doesn't make my body feel like it's being tortured would be good."

"Does reading in a tree count as an adventure or is that too tame?"

My heart tripped over itself before beating faster as if to make up for the mistake.

"That sounds wonderful." And although I tried to keep my tone light, even I could hear the slight breathlessness to it.

"Next week? Same time, same place?"

And when I nodded, it felt like something bigger.

Week 4

Excitement and nervousness warred in my body, creating a jitteriness deep in my bones — as if I couldn't even walk properly, let alone climb a tree. I gripped the book I'd brought and marched determinedly across the park. I didn't know what to expect — how to plan or control this — and it was equal parts terrifying and wonderful.

Ben was waiting for me in the tree, as he had been for the last two weeks, and I smiled at him, even though it felt stretched and weird. He reached down, his long fingers wrapping around mine as he helped me up, the muscles in his arms bunching in a way that made me want to wrap my hand around them.

He'd moved further up the branch, leaving me to sit snugly in the fork of the tree.

"I've taken your spot."

The twist of his mouth inspired the same movement in my stomach. "I'm happy to give it up."

"Oh," I said, unable to look away from those perfect lips. "Okay. Thanks."

He smiled, and my stomach did an extra twist for good measure. "Absolutely my pleasure."

I cleared my throat, totally out of my depth. "What now?"

"Now, we read."

"Right, of course." I opened my book — one I'd been meaning to read for ages — but the words may as well have been written in a different language for all the sense they made. I was distracted by the barest distance between his leg and mine; the thought that if I just moved slightly, our bodies would touch; the sound of his breathing; the smell of him.

When I'd read the same paragraph three times and still didn't know what it said, I looked up. He wasn't even pretending to read — his deliciously brown eyes were watching me and the jolt of desire that brought felt like it was almost big enough to knock me out of the tree.

"You're not reading." The desire flavoured my tone.

He tilted his head slightly. "I thought I wanted things that brought me happiness in the past, but it turns out new possibilities of pleasure are much more enthralling."

"Almost like a new adventure," I said, my voice just above a whisper.

"Exactly like that," he said, and he leant forward, giving me plenty of time to say no or turn my head. But I did neither. Instead, I leant forward too.

His lips touched mine, whisper soft — a teasing taste. Then firmer, more insistent, although I wasn't sure if that was him or me. I breathed into the kiss, my lips parting slightly and his tongue slid against mine, as if he was savouring the flavour of me. His hand cupped the side of my jaw, tracing the line of it, following the curve of my neck, my nerve endings anticipating every touch. I was addictively overwhelmed by him — his touch, his smell, his taste. So much so that when he pulled back, I forgot for a moment where I was. There was just him.

We sat in silence, looking at each other, our hands entwined.

"I like reading in trees," I said and thrilled at the fact I could make him laugh.

"I bought you something." He reached further up the tree, to a cooler bag I hadn't noticed wedged in another fork. "Ice-cream. *Sweet Pleasures*, in fact."

I licked my lips and it had nothing to do with the thought of ice-cream and everything to do with the remembered taste of his lips.

"Oh. Have I convinced you to try it?"

He didn't answer, instead taking the lid off the container and digging a spoon in. He held it out to me, his eyes daring me to taste. With deliberate slowness, in a way that made me feel decidedly Goddess-like, I took the spoon in my mouth, the sweetness dissolving on my tongue.

His small intake of breath made me feel... adventurous.

"Zesty lime and raspberry," he said, as if the words had to fight their way out of a tight chest.

"Delicious."

"Yes," he said, but he wasn't looking at the ice-cream. "Inspired by you."

I'm sure my confusion showed through my smile. "What?"

"*Sweet Pleasures*," he said. "It's my company. The changes I've had in the last six months."

I laughed. "Really?"

He nodded and took the paper bag from around the tub, displaying the name. *Adventure-seeking Goddess*.

And it felt like I was.

4

CLOSING THE DISTANCE

BRIDGET W DEEN

W e've been doing this dance for weeks now. Standing against the railing overlooking the Gap, pretending we don't seek each other out every Tuesday, Thursday, and Saturday afternoon at 5:00 pm. Today though... today is different.

For one, I'm not holding on to any crutches. I'm standing on my own. He isn't dressed in his gym gear either. He's wearing casual clothes that fit his frame nicely, a pair of black-rimmed glasses on his nose and a soft serve in his free hand. He hasn't eaten it yet. Finn, his energetic golden retriever, is about ready to pounce and swallow it in one bite.

My leg begins to burn from the build-up of lactic acid, a result of standing too long and walking too far without help. It feels good. It feels bad. I feel tired.

I tear my eyes away from the fading sun and decide to take a seat on one of the long wooden benches, finding a spot beside a few couples sitting to watch the sunset. The late autumn wind is chilly, flinging the ends of my hair over my shoulders and against my cheeks. With stiff fingers, I massage my thigh over my pants, stopping at the place where my right leg ends and my prosthetic one begins.

The waves crash a resounding chorus along the cliffs in front of me, and as I hold my palms against the cool metal, I wish the water could soothe me as it once did. But even though my body is recovering, returning to moving with some sense of normality, my mind is still far, far behind.

In the corner of my eye, I can see my observer wrangling Finn to sit and be still. The dog is too excited by the ice cream dripping down his owner's hand and the screech of young children riding scooters along the stone walkway to pay attention.

My lips curl up in amusement. He looks over to me sitting on the bench and smirks back, embarrassment clear in the hitch of his shoulders. I hold his stare for a beat before I return my attention to the sea, breathe in its salty scent, and try to rid my mind of the horribly disjointed memories that swamp me every time anything blue or grey or wet comes into my field of vision.

I glance back to see my very familiar stranger has finally got Finn under control and they're striding over to my bench. I smile again when I realise I know the dog's name but not his.

He takes a seat beside me and begins to let Finn lick the ice cream. I laugh at the absurdity of the dog's tongue, the desperation in his eyes.

My stranger glances at me and laughs along too. Then he says, "So, you got a new leg, huh?" And a bubble of air in the shape of a laugh bursts from my throat. I can't stop it; I can't shove it back down. The comment is so unexpected and so genuine and so *not* what I thought he would say that I can't contain the surprise.

And what's even more odd... I'm laughing for the first time beside the ocean since the day it ruined my life.

෨෨

Her laughter is better than I expected. It's easy and rich and I'm pretty sure she hides a snort at one point. I didn't think my question would get this reaction. I'm not sure if the laughter is covering the fact that it was rude or if it upset her. Maybe I shouldn't have been so bold. But as the seconds tick by, I don't regret it. She's smiling and laughing. I've never seen her do that before and it's... amazing.

I hope she doesn't think I'm some kind of stalker. But it's impossible not to notice that she's walking on her own. Her amputated leg is now sporting a new prosthetic. I can see the metal joint where her ankle should be. The independence has made her appear stronger, but it wasn't until my stupid comment that she actually looks at ease. It suits her, this happy state, and it's far better than the shell of a woman I saw all those weeks ago.

Since that first long-distance encounter, I've learnt three things about her. One: she's traumatised, scared, but she hides behind a steeled expression that does a good job of making it look like she's coping. Two: she lost a part of herself and comes here every Tuesday, Thursday, and Saturday afternoon to find it again. I don't think she's discovered it yet, but she's trying. Three: she's always on her own, like a soldier facing down an army with only a gun and a single bullet.

I'm so distracted watching her that I don't realise Finn has devoured the soft serve and is now trying to swallow my hand. I wipe my hands as best I can on my jeans and give his head a pat, smiling wide for his muddy brown eyes to see. Content with having found every last remnant of sugar, he turns his attention to her, rubbing up against her black tracksuit pants and leaving a carpet of golden fur in his wake.

"I'm sorry, he's very social," I say.

Her laughter dies a little, but her smile widens as she begins to stroke Finn. "Aren't you a good boy Finnie! Did you like your treat?" Finn's tail wags as he sits himself between her legs, looking out to the ocean, enjoying her fingers scratching his back. "He's so soft."

"Yeah, it's nice until you have to vacuum six times a day." That comment gets another laugh from her. I should be keeping score of how many she gives me. Like a kid collecting Pokémon cards, stashing them away like some sort of treasure.

"Have you met many golden retrievers named Finn?" I ask.

"Aren't they all called Finn?" she responds, and I chuckle a little at her question. She's not wrong. My sister couldn't have picked a more basic name. No offence to any human Finns.

"He likes you," I say, trying to keep the conversation flowing.

She smiles and continues to stroke Finn's back. Every second stroke she lets his long hair untangle from her fingers and float into the wind. "Golden retrievers like everyone."

"True. Have you had one?"

"No. I used to have a cattle dog, but he died a year ago."

"Damn. That sucks."

"Yeah," she says, and I feel like there's so much weight in that one word. "I'm Kita, by the way." Suddenly she seems more real than ever before.

"Jason."

She smiles at me. "Nice to finally meet you." I know what she means by that.

"It's good to meet you too, Kita."

⁶⁸²⁰

My name shouldn't sound that nice slipping through someone's lips. But it does. Jason makes it sound nice. Like it's more than just a four-letter word, with two syllables. It's an entire galaxy. A person.

I lean back, wipe my hands free of Finn's fur and tuck them under my bum. Jason watches me as if he's worried I'll walk away. I won't. This moment has been building for a long time. Weeks of watching him run along this walkway, making quick eye contact and cataloguing his every move has finally led to this. To him, being bold enough to shatter the fragile wall between us.

I'm grateful he finally did because I'm not sure if I ever would have.

I come here to try and feel peaceful again, but all it does is choke me up. Suffocate me. For months, people have told me I'm strong. I'm yet to feel even an ounce of it.

"Not running today?" I ask.

"Injured my back earlier in the week. Walking is all I can do for a while," he says and then he opens his mouth as if he could lasso his words and pull them back down his throat. "Not that walking is bad or anything."

I laugh. I can't help it. He asked me about my leg quite boldly and then thinks talking about being restricted to walking is bad. "It's alright. I get it." I reach down and flick my fingers against my metal leg. The tiny *ting* is muffled by the crash of the waves and the whip of the wind.

He smiles, somewhat relieved. I stare at him openly now. His glasses hide his thick eyebrows, but I know the shape of them already. Like I also know his features hint at First Nations heritage, his eyes are the colour of freshly brewed coffee, and his teeth are a little crooked, but bright and beautiful. He's utterly gorgeous and the butterflies that sprung to life the first time we made eye contact, suddenly begin to flutter anew as I realise he's sitting right beside me.

"So, what do you do when you're not running?" I ask. He straightens his glasses. "I like the glasses, by the way."

He huffs at my comment.

"Thanks. Finn ate my last pair of contacts." I shake my head at Finn, who is too busy watching the birds in the distance to notice.

Jason continues, "I'm a primary school teacher. You?"

"I work part time as a receptionist for a Pilates studio. I train for my swimming every other day. *Used* to, anyway." He nods but doesn't add anything more. I get it. He doesn't want to bring up why I don't train anymore. It's so blatantly obvious.

"When do you think you'll get back to it?" he asks and this time I'm left genuinely shocked. Most of the responses I get when people hear what happened to me are not *that*. Most people dodge and weave around the subject of getting back to training, like even mentioning that I used to swim long distance in the ocean will cause me to break down.

"I'm still trying to figure it out," I reply. Because I am. But, I'm also not. He doesn't push, and the weighted silence has me opening up. "I can't go to the beach anymore, not after the attack. Just looking at the sand makes me..." My good leg begins to bounce, Finn lies down and rests his head on my prosthetic foot. "This is as close to the ocean as I want to get."

Jason looks out to the sea and the darkening sky, and then back at me. "You'll get there." He says it with such certainty I feel like I could lie in the pool of his confidence.

"Thanks."

Jason shifts, blocking the wind that has begun to numb my cheeks. I'm grateful that he's so observant. I want to lean into his warmth. "Is there a reason you come alone?" he asks, gentle.

"I just need some space." I sigh, all the tension in my chest unravelling like it never has before. "My family has been amazing since the attack. They try to sympathise with what I'm going through; they listen to the psychologists on how to deal with me. But it's too much sometimes. I just need to be alone, and I guess facing my fear at the same time works out well."

This is the first time I've said those words aloud.

No-one can relate to what it feels like choking on salt water mixed with your own blood, to feel your leg pop off and your skin ripped to shreds, to think you're going to die lying on the wet sand you once loved more than your own bed. To see your dream drift away with the receding of the tide, as if it never existed in the first place.

They try to. Understand, that is. But it's impossible, and the overbearing weight of everyone's sympathy makes me angry. It makes me feel like the shark not only stole my life, but my humanity as well.

"That seems fair," he says and again, I'm shocked and confused and leaning into him. No, literally, my shoulder is against his. Did he move or did I?

⊗

I moved. I can't explain what drove me. Maybe it was the fact that she was answering my questions. Maybe it was the fact that she was speaking so calmly about her situation; the need to comfort her was like a primal instinct. Or maybe it was because she had moved first. Just an inch. Enough for me to notice that my body wasn't so far away anymore.

We're both silent for another minute, content to watch the bruised sky bleed pink and orange in the distance.

Kita speaks first, "Did you buy Finn an ice cream cone on purpose?" I turn to see her expression isn't so pinched.

"Is it weird if I say yes?"

"No," she says, her green-blue eyes running over my face. "I don't come alone, you know."

"What do you mean?" I ask, shifting completely to face her.

"Well, maybe the first afternoon, yeah. But every other day... you've been here." Her lips peel back into a shy smile, and it makes me want to bury my face in her neck. "I guess what I'm trying to say is... thanks for looking out for me. For sitting with me."

I reach for her hand. Her cheeks turn rosy pink and I feel her body still. She lets me intertwine my fingers with hers, press my palm to her palm. She's warm against my skin.

I don't know how I'm supposed to let go.

∞

I've been touched every day, constantly for months. Doctors, family, friends, nurses. Each one helped to steady me, to comfort me, to heal me.

But this... Jason's palm? It ignites something shiny inside of me and lets it loose to run down a sparkling red carpet straight to my heart.

He runs his thumb along the back of my hand, and I melt into him. Quietly, he shifts his body so that our shoulders are touching. I can feel his thigh against mine, but not his calf or his knee or his ankle. He keeps my hand in his, Finn's lead in the other. Soon, our breaths sync in time with each other as we watch the sun disappear for the night and bathe the Gap in blissful darkness.

Minutes later, I can't see the ocean anymore.

"I once heard something about if you have bad memories tied to a certain place, a good way to ease them is to create new, happy memories to overlap them," he says. The only thing moving is his thumb on my hand and Finn's chest against my other leg. "I don't know if it works as easy as that, but I can understand the idea."

My head falls onto his shoulder. It fits perfectly. "Makes sense. But yeah, I don't know if it works like that."

"Did knowing I was here make it easier for you to come to the Gap?" he asks quietly. Curious.

"Yeah, it did."

"I wonder if you went to the beach, to look for someone in particular, if that would ease the tension." He pauses. "Maybe I could meet you there."

I lift my head from his shoulder to look him right in the eyes. "You would do that for me? As a total stranger."

"You're not a stranger anymore, Kita."

I'm breathless. The wind steals the oxygen right out of my mouth and won't give it back. Jason drops the lead in his hand to squish between his knees and then he's pushing my wild hair back behind my ears.

His hand pauses to cup my chin. "But yes. I would do that. Of course, I would." He smiles again and I want to take a picture of him. Then he just looks ashamed and says, "I gave Finn ice cream knowing he would have catastrophic diarrhoea in the morning, just so I could find something to talk to you about."

We burst out laughing.

ೞ

"Oh no, Finnie!" she says and rubs her hands into his fur. Finn stirs from his position on the floor to stand up and look at us both.

Kita's laughter surrounds me and without thinking, I lean in close to her. She finds my gaze and I'm positive she can read what's on my mind. I hope it's not obvious. Too pushy for someone she's just met.

"Jason?" Her voice is breathy, soft. My lungs no longer know how to function.

"Yeah?"

"Can you take me to the beach someday?" Something deep inside me cracks open at how brave she is.

"Anytime, just say the word," I say, and she leans in. Closer. Her nose is pink from the cold. I let go of her hand to place both of my palms either side of her cheeks. Her eyelids grow heavy, slow blinking.

"Kita?" She lifts her eyebrows in answer. "Can I kiss you now?" She nods, one hand wraps around my wrist, the other lands lightly on my shoulder. I press my lips to hers tenderly, carefully. She's soft and shaking and my heart pounds against my ribcage as if to say, *yes, yes, she's perfect, don't let her go.*

附

"Did you want to get something to eat?" Jason asks and my beaming smile is enough of a response for him. We stand, Finn's tail wagging his excitement. I take Jason's free hand and he waits patiently for me to move.

We walk along the path at a slow pace, and I feel like I'm dreaming. But I'm not, because the ocean waves hitting the cliffs keep calling out for my attention.

And this time, instead of saying no,

I say... *soon.*

5
OPERATION FIVE-GALLON TIN

FIONA M MARSDEN

North Queensland. New Year's Eve 1944

A flicker of light showed a figure beyond the neat row of Willys MB Jeeps parked alongside the administration block of the hospital. David doused his torch. If someone else was here, he'd have to hold off. He strained to see the illuminated dial of his watch under the leather casing. He'd hoped to be back before the change of shift. The night nurses always did their rounds when they came on duty at eleven.

"Are you going to wait all night, soldier?" A torchlight, the beam confined to a narrow strip by tape, flicked off the ground and landed in his face.

Sprung.

"Sister Williams?" He squinted against the light and she lowered it.

She came forward, skirting one of the ambulances, the light from her torch reflecting up from the bare dirt. "Sergeant Mallings. Shouldn't you be safely tucked up in bed?"

Lieutenant Nancy Williams wasn't in her usual nurse's kit. Tonight, she sported a pair of khaki trousers tied at the ankles to keep out the nasty bugs of which there were plenty in North Queensland. Her trim figure looked good in the matching long-sleeved blouse, and her wide-brimmed uniform hat showed more of her pale blonde hair than was usually seen under the veils the sisters wore in the wards. A gas mask bag hung from one shoulder with her steel helmet hooked on the outside. She looked marginally more approachable in this gear, even with the holstered .45 on her hip.

"You look ready for anything. Are you here to arrest me or return me to the ward?"

"I'm here to escort you on your mission, soldier. A man recuperating from malaria with a dodgy knee and recently dislocated shoulder is probably unsafe on the roads at night."

"My superiors obviously don't agree. I'm being shipped out tomorrow."

She indicated the nearest Jeep. "Your carriage awaits."

Curious at her attitude, David clambered in, not bothering to clip the side rope in place. "Isn't this against the rules?"

"I'm an officer, soldier." She tossed her mask and helmet into the back seat and joined him in the vehicle. "The rules are in my favour."

"I meant the rules about fraternisation, Lieutenant."

"This isn't fraternisation. I'm transporting a patient. But you can call me Nancy for tonight." She stomped on the starter and adjusted the choke when the engine roared into life. Her hand brushed against his bare leg below his shorts as she changed gears and spun out onto the road. David forced himself not to flinch.

"Where are we going? The MP's offices are in the other direction."

"I understood the target was the officers' mess at Hoevet Field, this side of Mareeba."

"Do you have spies in the wards?"

She laughed. "With canvas walls and nurses popping in and out, you can't keep any secrets from us, soldier."

The laugh was a honeyed sound that ripped through his gut. The likes of her weren't for a non-comm. Everyone knew Nancy Williams was a favourite with the doctors and commissioned officers. She was so damned beautiful with her blue-eyed, pin-up-girl style. Even now, with only a slash of red lipstick, she was a killer for looks.

His gaze dropped to the pistol on her hip. "Where'd you get the gun?"

"It's from when I was posted to New Guinea. I was at Nadzab for a while with the American girls."

"It's a wonder we didn't meet up there. I was in hospital a couple of times. Nothing serious."

She cocked her head, her brows raised before returning her focus to the road. The blackout lights weren't great but with a waning full moon the visibility could be worse.

He decided to answer the unspoken question. She was a nurse, of course she was curious about why he'd been hospitalised. There was no future for them, but there was tonight. "I arrived back from the Middle East in time to relieve at Kokoda. Had my first bout of malaria, which knocked me for six, and re-joined my unit in time for the offensive at Shaggy Ridge. Been all over the place since."

Changing gear, she slowed the Jeep. "I was probably up there while you were in the field. They had to ship me back after a rotten case of dengue fever."

"I'm not sure which is worse. Had a mate with typhus. Nearly killed him. We all got the trots at one time or another." He grabbed at the handrail as they swung off the main road. "Bloody war."

"I know."

Her hand left the steering wheel for a moment, resting lightly on his knee. It sent shocks through his system. This close, he was aware of her subtle scent, sweet and floral with a medicinal undertone.

The lights of the airfield glowed in the sky ahead. No blackout tonight. A couple of U.S. marked Jeeps were bouncing along the dirt road in front of them, overloaded with airmen. Nancy swung in behind them, matching speed. "Perfect."

Her confidence buoyed his own. "You think we'll get past the guards this way?"

"It's New Year's Eve. There's a dance tonight at the hall in Tolga. Most of the officers and men will be out flirting with the local girls. I doubt they'll be checking too closely on a few Jeeps. Besides there are a bunch of our guys posted here at the moment, prepping to head north."

She would have heard the chatter from the senior officers at the hospital.

The paddock to the left of them was closed off with fences heavy with barbed wire. A reconnaissance aircraft was coming in to land, the lights along the air strip barely visible from this distance.

He jerked forward as the vehicles in front braked and Nancy did the same. It reminded him painfully that his knee was still not fully healed.

"Did I jar your leg?"

"It's fine."

He resisted the urge to rub away the ache. Pride, of course. Which was stupid. She'd seen him writhing in agony and burning up with a fever. Pointless trying to pretend to be some kind of hero now.

The soldiers at the gate waved the Jeeps through with barely a look.

Nancy slowed, breaking away from the mini convoy. "Where to from here, soldier?"

"Over near the admin offices."

"Behind the officers' mess. You've done your homework."

"You seem to know where everything is."

"I've been doing my own reconnaissance." She grinned at him as she brought the Jeep to a halt in the shadows away from the airfield. "I was invited to a Christmas Party here by the officers."

His heart sank to his already churning gut. Of course, she'd have been here. The Yanks appreciated a beautiful woman when they saw one.

"Will you be alright while I go in?"

"Go ahead, soldier. I'm a big girl. I can take care of myself."

ᏰᏗᏁᎧ

Nancy watched the sergeant slink off into the shadows. He didn't need camouflage gear. After hours sunbaking while they recuperated, most of the fellows were nut-brown, darker even than their uniforms. With his dark hair and eyes, he blended perfectly.

She couldn't help liking David Mallings. He was a real gentleman. Even when he'd been in agony after they removed the shrapnel lodged in his thigh and the pieces of shattered patella, he'd managed to thank everyone.

If his eyes had lingered a little longer on her, she couldn't read anything into it. Most of the soldiers claimed to have fallen for one or more of the nurses. They were incorrigible flirts, the lot of them. After years at war, they hadn't been home to sweethearts or wives for a long time. Nurses were often the only women they'd seen for months on end by the time they turned up in hospital.

Yet there was something about Sergeant Mallings. He was a genuine hero, not that he'd said anything. Typical of Aussie soldiers who would rather put themselves down than own up to doing something brave. It had been another member of his unit who'd told the tale of how the sergeant had saved him and three other men, at the cost of his own injury.

David always laughed off any comments, telling the others to deal the cards or shut up. He'd told her, early on, how he'd managed to hold onto the greasy pack of cards right from the time he left home. He spent hours playing patience once he was able to sit up, the fever settled.

A sound alerted her to a movement in the darkness and she leaned against the Willys, trying to look bored. An airman and one of the nurses from the U.S. Hospital. Nancy dug out a pack of cigarettes from a box in the back of the Jeep and casually lit one.

"Nice evening, ma'am." The young airman had a distinctive accent, probably from the south.

She offered them cigarettes. "A little warm for my liking, but I'm guessing you'd be used to it."

She exchanged a few more observations on the weather while they puffed and then the youngster gave a nod and they wandered off, probably to find more comfortable quarters.

"Have they gone?"

David stepped out of the darkness and she extinguished the cigarette in the dirt. "Good timing."

"I've been here a couple of minutes." He rolled across a large cylindrical parcel. Nancy helped him stow it in the back, pulling a piece of the canvas canopy over it. It was bloody heavy.

"I take it the mission was successful."

"So far. Now we need to get back to Rocky Creek quick smart."

He climbed into the Jeep with a wide grin. "Home James, and don't spare the horsepower."

His euphoria was catching. In minutes they were out of the gates and heading back along the Atherton Road towards the hospital. Once they'd settled into a steady forty miles an hour, she relaxed a little.

"You said you were being shipped out tomorrow. Where to?"

"No orders yet, but I'm guessing Borneo or points north. We may have them on the run from New Guinea but there's still a lot of ground to cover."

"What will you do after?"

He was silent for a few minutes. "I haven't really thought about it much. It's easier to take each day as it comes. Once you start thinking of home, you get distracted, lose your edge."

"Where is home? Do you have family?"

"A little country town you've likely never heard of. Plenty of family. I have a stack of brothers and sisters." He rubbed his knee absently. "My brothers are a lot younger. I used to resent it, thought they were spoiled by my parents and my sisters. Now I'm glad. They're both too young for the war, though Bill will be eighteen next August. He'll join up for sure."

"Maybe it'll be over by then."

"I'm not counting on it. When we shipped out in thirty-nine, we were worried it would be over before we arrived. Stupid kids we were. Didn't want to miss the fun."

"How old were you? You'd have had to be over twenty in 1940 to go to Palestine and Tobruk."

"Close enough. All my mates were going, and they were older. We went together to sign up and the army didn't question it."

She wondered how old he was now. She'd met a fellow who would have been seventeen when he signed up but he'd put his age up by six months so he could join with his brothers. "I'd done my nursing training, so I was twenty-one when I shipped out to Singapore in 1940."

He was staring. She could feel his gaze boring into her.

"That must have been tough."

Such simple words yet they soothed a heart still aching from the loss of so many friends. The shame of surviving, not knowing their fate. She forced a smile. "You have more family than me. I'm technically an orphan. Brought up by my Gran."

"Is she still alive?"

"Yes. She doesn't remember me. My uncle put her in a hospital while I was in training. The staff are kind to her."

"If you want family, I've got plenty to share. Even a full complement of grandparents."

Her breath caught. She forced herself to keep it light. "That would be a treat. Maybe I'll take you up on that."

The Jeep shuddered to a halt as she pulled up outside the wards. It looked like he was about to say something, but a group of men were watching from one of the wards, the canvas sides rolled up to keep cool.

"Hey Mallings, you manage to get hold of it?"

David heaved up the parcel and there was a massive cheer. Nurses and patients came pouring out of other parts of the hospital to find out what was happening.

A couple of the other patients came to relieve him of the parcel.

He scrambled onto the back of the Jeep. "Ice-cream for everyone, courtesy of our Yankee allies."

The crowd swarmed inside with the five-gallon tin of ice-cream, demanding plates and spoons, leaving the two of them alone.

He climbed down and faced her. "Happy New Year, Nancy Williams."

"May it be a good one, David Mallings."

He saluted her and stepped away. "I'll be seeing you."

She watched him join his fellow patients, swallowed up in their congratulations and comradery.

"I'll be seeing you too, soldier."

ᏻᏮᎨᎧ

The train jerked as it chugged slowly into the station. It had been more than six long years since he'd been in his hometown. A crowd gathered on the platform, and he'd lay money they weren't all here to meet family and friends. The twice weekly arrivals had always brought half the town to watch when he was a child. The engine might fascinate the children but for the adults it was blatant curiosity.

There wouldn't be anyone to meet him.

He hadn't written to his family to let them know his arrival date. He dreaded any kind of welcome home parade. Steadying himself on the open window ledge, he pulled down a small suitcase from the rack. It was light enough. A change of underwear and a pair of freshly bought pyjamas jostled with his shaving gear and a few keepsakes from his time in the army. His pack of cards.

It still felt strange to be in civvies, wearing a suit he'd probably only have a use for twice a year. The squeal of brakes warned him to brace himself again and he used the door into the corridor. It reminded him to grab his walking stick from the seat. *Damn knee.* The army sawbones said he'd always have a limp because the bullet had aggravated the old injury from Shaggy Ridge.

He followed his fellow passengers to the exit, stumbling at the long step down to the platform.

With luck there might be someone he knew who could give him a ride across the creek to his family's property.

The sea of faces was overwhelming after his last stint at the rehab hospital in Brisbane. A blonde head of hair, neatly coiled, caught his eye above a shapely figure in a snug white dress splotched with strawberries. His chest tightened. It had been months since he'd had a letter from Nancy. Not since he'd written to tell her he'd always be a bit of a crock.

All the same, he kept his eye on the girl. She was looking for someone, bobbing up and down to see over the moving crowd. His breath stalled as she turned his way. *It couldn't be.* Her blue eyes widened, and her berry-red lips curved up in a smile. He stood frozen as she dodged around a family group and stood in front of him.

He choked out the question buzzing in his brain. "Nancy Williams? What are you doing here?"

"I'm assistant matron at the hospital." Her smile faltered. "Didn't you get my letter?"

"I haven't heard from you since you said you were demobbed and heading south to see your gran." It was probably still following him around. He'd been all over the place since Borneo. Three different hospitals in three countries and then rehab.

"It doesn't matter. You're here now." She tweaked her gloves. "Unless you aren't pleased to see me?"

"Hell, Nancy. There's no-one I wanted to see more."

"That's all right then. Would you like a ride home?"

"Do you have time?"

"I'm not on duty until tomorrow, so I'm all yours."

He wished.

Taking his case, she tucked her arm through his and he went with her in a dream. Her warmth came through the fabric of the coat, unfreezing his chest. "How did you know I was coming?"

She flashed a smile. "I've been coming to meet every train when I'm off-duty."

He halted with a jolt as they reached the street. "You're driving a Willys. Again?"

"The army were selling them at a good price. Otherwise, they would have let them rust somewhere. You know the army."

She tossed his case into the back and climbed into the driver's seat, tucking in her skirts. "Are you coming?"

With a laugh, he joined her. "Where are we going?"

She looked him up and down. "You look warmish. How about we stop at the café and have an ice-cream sundae?"

"You know I'll go anywhere for ice-cream, so long as you're with me." It was the most natural thing in the world to lean across and kiss her. She tasted of berries and warm summer sun.

"I can see I'll have to keep my makeup kit handy."

Her eyes were tender, belying her smart comment.

He cupped her cheek. "I love you, Nancy Williams."

"I love you too, soldier."

She pressed the starter and he settled back in his seat. It might occasionally be a bumpy ride, but he knew the journey would be extraordinary.

6

MISS MARCHANT'S MERRIMENT

CHELSEA LOCKE

*T*he Hon Alicia Marchant

Miss Marchant,

I feel it is only fitting to correct your disparagement of hollyhocks yesterday when we met at Gunter's Tea Rooms. You may indeed be correct when declaring your triumph as the most successful wallflower of the 1816 Season. I'm no expert on such matters, but to compare yourself to a tall skinny hollyhock is maligning the graceful elegance of this beautiful flower and, dare I say, you.

Please enjoy the strawberries; may they remind you of your first taste of ice cream. It was my pleasure to meet you. I enjoyed my short time with you and my sister Harriet. I hope we meet again soon.

Yours

Rochford

Alicia could barely take in what she was reading for all the chatter from the servants. The first gift she'd received since this wretched time in London had begun. Her heart soared on the charming, almost playful, tone of the note. Really at the age of seven and twenty, she should be past succumbing to flattery from a handsome gentleman with twinkling green eyes.

"What's all this?" came the soft query from her brother.

"A gift from someone I met yesterday."

Martin smiled on seeing the flowers. "Hollyhocks are an unusual choice of flowers. I'd have thought lilies more appropriate."

Alicia smiled, deciding not to comment. He was readying himself for the day in Parliament. After her brother's inheritance of the lands and title of Baron of Marchant from a distant family member who failed in producing an heir, their lives had changed overnight, rescuing them from genteel poverty. Martin was determined to use his new position to better the lives of Waterloo veterans.

"So, Lissy, who is your admirer?"

Alicia smiled at Martin's pet name for her and set about correcting him. "Not an admirer. A simple gift from Viscount Rochford, Harriet's brother, whom I met yesterday when I visited Gunter's Tea Rooms."

Martin's expression turned thunderous, his face flushing a vivid deep ruby plum. Alicia startled when he began shouting, sending the servants scurrying.

"Rochford is not a suitable acquaintance, and I insist you avoid him during your time in London."

Martin's plump face now resembled an overripe plum. Given her new fascination with ice cream, she wondered if plums would make lovely ices. They produced delicious jam, so surely they would combine perfectly with cream and sugar?

"I hope he doesn't plan to court you."

Alicia laughed. "Oh Martin, I've no interest in a courtship that might lead to a marriage."

Taken aback, Martin was silent for a moment. "Not want marriage? Impossible."

Alicia collected her reticule in preparation to leave. "Not impossible, Martin. Why would I give up my freedom to have my every moment, to quote the Bard, 'cabined cribbed confined' by a husband?" She dusted her hands in a dismissive gesture. "No, thank you."

ぐった

Tucked up beside a large palm, Alicia knew she'd been foolish to attend the Ferncourt Ball. All for the chance to meet Ferncourt's son, Viscount Rochford, again.

A palm frond twitched. She looked up to see smiling moss-green eyes. "Good evening, Miss Marchant."

"Lord Rochford, why are you hiding behind a palm?"

"Well, I'm looking for the wallflower of the Season. Have you by chance seen her?"

Alicia laughed. "I can see my choice of words is going to haunt me, sir."

He moved around the palm and stood before her. "Perhaps," he teased. "May I have this next dance?"

"That, sir, might be hazardous. There are many debutantes and anxious mamas who would see you dance and assume you're seeking a wife."

Rochford nodded ruefully. "It is my sorry lot in life to arouse excitement in the bosoms of mothers, to no avail." He extended his gloved hand. "My attention has been captured by a rare and charming self-proclaimed wallflower." He smiled. "A description I disagree with most fervently."

Clasping her hand, and with an elegant low bow, he said "Please, Miss Marchant, do me the honour of this waltz." Rochford's hand lingered, setting off tiny bursts of unexpected desire and longing. Such lovely sensations skittered through her. She looked into those sparkling eyes and suspected he may be experiencing the same feelings.

Alicia smiled. This dance would be like strawberry ice cream. Magical.

Rochford's hand rested lightly on her waist, and the resulting tingle could only be described as astonishing. Never had a partner's touch set off such a reaction, buoyancy bubbling and fizzing from tip to toe. They began to circle the floor, avoiding the masses clustering in the centre and weaving their way around the edges. Soon their movements were in perfect accord. Alicia gave over to the pleasure and thrill of dancing with an attractive, accomplished partner.

"May I call you Alicia?"

He skilfully guided them around a boisterous couple. "And please call me Rochford or Daniel." Alicia considered the request.

"You may call me Alicia." She tapped him slightly, enjoying the strength below her touch.

Alicia wondered how Martin would feel about their rapid move into familiarity. But then, little did she care. The exaggerated courtesy and formality of the London Season were exhausting and tedious compared to her previous life. Plus, she'd so few friends in London she couldn't afford to be cavalier in her rejections. They danced on, oblivious to their surroundings. Had she paid attention to her fellow guests, she would have seen them with mouths agape, whispering and gossiping behind fans as they watched her glide gracefully with Rochford around the magnificent room.

The orchestra played the final notes, and they came to a stop. Rochford extended an arm. "May I escort you to supper?"

Alicia, while tempted, knew it would set tongues wagging. "Thank you, but no. My brother will be escorting me."

Rochford's face fell, and her breath hitched at having to refuse. Martin arrived at her side, offering Rochford a dismissive nod as he led her away.

"The man certainly looks like he is beginning a courtship."

Alicia gusted a soft laugh. "Oh, Martin, it was a waltz, not a declaration."

"Perhaps, all the same, he should have approached me for my consent."

"Martin, I'm well past the age of needing your consent." She patted his arm in a conciliatory move. "Please don't make more of this than an offer of friendship on his part."

Some fifteen minutes later, she was more than ready to escape the supper room and the curious looks from fellow guests. It would seem her escape from anonymity was causing talk.

"Excuse me, Miss Marchant."

Alicia looked up to see a young servant in Ferncourt livery standing behind her chair. She smiled. "Yes?" He bent forward and set a tiny glass bowl before her.

"Viscount Rochford sends you this pineapple ice with his compliments."

Alicia looked around for the man making such a bold gesture. Dear me, more tongues wagging and one very annoyed brother. But still, she found herself unable to suppress a smile in the direction of Rochford, who leant negligently against a far wall returning her smile

"No!" someone gasped. "Pineapple? I've heard of the fruit, but never tasted it."

Alicia was at a loss for words. It would appear she'd be singled out for this special treat.

"My, you have attracted the attention of Viscount Rochford this evening," sniped a young woman sitting across from her.

Deciding not to rise to the spite in the comment, she responded gently. "Yes, Rochford knows that I'm an enthusiast of Mr Gunter's confections." Alicia spooned the cold, sweet concoction into her mouth. She relished the burst of sunshine tickling on her tongue. It was the only way to describe the fresh summery taste. As she savoured, she knew Rochford watched her luxuriate with every mouthful. His pleasure in her pleasure was again unmistakable.

"We'll be leaving now, Alicia," announced Martin as he glared across the room at Rochford, who responded with an amicable toast of his wine glass. A low growl was Martin's only response. Again, she wondered why Martin so disliked Rochford. Plus, she had matters to consider. Rochford was telling the world he planned to court her. She had to decide if she welcomed his clear intentions. Perhaps she did wish to be 'cabined, cribbed and confined'?

༼༺༻༽

"Viscount Rochford asks if you're at home?" queried a servant.

Last night had been long and sleepless as she mulled over how to respond to Rochford's attentions, but early that morning, she had made her decision. No-one was more surprised than her.

"Yes, I'm at home." The footman exited. She tilted her head to hear Rochford's arrival and listened to his firm steps moving up the staircase. He strode into the morning room and made his bow, followed by a wide easy smile. His dark hair was swept back, curling softly around his upturned collar, his cravat in the mathematical style, his trousers a soft cream. Hessian boots glinted, suggesting hard work and champagne by an attentive valet. His shirt was of a soft white muslin, accented by a waistcoat in a simple cream with a gold thread woven throughout. And all this splendour was topped off with a tailcoat cropped at the front.

"Good morning, Alicia." He chose to ignore the chair Alicia indicated for him to sit in. Instead, he sat beside her on the settee with a flip of his tails. He lifted her hand to his lips. "I've come to ask if you would enjoy a carriage ride in Hyde Park?"

"You're very bold in your attentions, Rochford."

"Do you think?" He leaned back slightly to study her. "I won't lie. I enjoy your company, and I want to spend more time with you." A relaxed smile followed. "Therefore, a carriage ride followed by a visit to Gunter's Tea Rooms should provide ample opportunity."

Alicia's nature was adventurous, and what Rochford suggested sounded perfect. But she had misgivings. A brother who she loved made his distaste of Viscount Rochford evident. Was Rochford courting her, or was seduction the aim of all this attention? She looked at the wide-open door to the morning room and understood immediately this was no seduction.

Rochford seemed to understand her dilemma. "I see your hesitancy, and your brother's dislike of me weighs heavily on you." Alicia went to speak, but he lifted a finger to her lips. "I am wooing you. I respect you, and I want you to trust that I will make it right with your brother."

"Why are you at such odds with him?"

His reply surprised her. "I am not at odds with your brother." Ruefully, he added "Your brother has an opinion of what occurred during a major charge of the Horse Guards at Waterloo." He shook his head and his expression became distant. "It's not a story I have wanted to tell, but I fear it now needs to be told."

He held her hand once again and his sunny smile returned. "Do you trust me?"

"For the moment, yes."

"And will you go driving in Hyde Park with me this afternoon?"

"Yes. But no more ice cream. I have my figure to consider."

 handwick

Walking into the dining room of Carlton House, the heavy perfume from masses of flowers on every visible surface verged on overwhelming. As was the heat. She'd heard the Regent was wary of catching a chill, and Alicia wondered how the Prince of Wales' staff and friends endured it. She would do so for one night to support Martin, in the hope of easing their growing estrangement.

Over the past two weeks, Rochford had continued to seek her out at social events. Flowers and gifts arrived most days. Carriage rides in Hyde Park became a regular occurrence. And so, the estrangement between siblings grew. Alicia, well past the age of following orders from her brother, ignored all his demands to avoid Daniel.

How could she reject him? They enjoyed so many shared interests. The Theatre, country life over city life, games of chance, and more. After so many years of avoiding matrimony, she realised it wasn't marriage she avoided. It was the potential partner. Alicia could imagine a pleasing future with Rochford, but feared she may be forced to choose between him and her family. This evening offered a respite from the hard decisions looming. Tonight, Daniel would not be attending, she thought. Perhaps there would be an opportunity for Alicia and Martin to alleviate their growing divide. Martin, clearly in his element, viewed this invitation as an opportunity to advance his political aspirations.

As they were seated to dine, she saw Martin placed next to the Regent — indeed, an honour. Also, she suspected, an unusual break in protocol. She was seated halfway down the long dining table.

"Good evening, Alicia. You're looking beautiful tonight." Dismay battled with delight when she saw Rochford seated to her right.

"Oh, tosh!" Alicia knew too well she might be considered handsome but never beautiful. Her hair colour remained stubbornly fixed between blonde and brunette, to her frustration. Some may have described the colour as teak. To her, it could only ever be called a mousy brown.

"I didn't realise you would be a guest this evening." She looked up to see Martin glowering at them — no chance of peace this night.

"I need to clear up the misapprehension your brother has of me and my actions at Waterloo." He paused, taking a slow, steadying breath before continuing. "If I want us to be together."

Alicia's heart skipped. Then at least ten extra rapid fluttery beats. Could this really be happening?

She looked at Martin then back to Rochford. "But I don't understand why being here assists."

"You and Martin are close. You shouldn't have to choose between us. I need your brother to be happy for you."

"And how will dining at Carlton House tonight support your case?"

With a subtle nod towards the Regent, he turned to Alicia. "I planned never to marry. I had no interest in a marriage to increase wealth and produce the obligatory heir." His gaze never wavered from hers. "But one sunny day in Berkeley Square, while leaning against the railings ordering ice cream for my chattering sister, I met a woman who took my breath away. Hazel eyes laughed as she tasted ice cream for the first time. She talked with ease and wit. No airs and graces. No attempts to lure flattery from me. Just simple enjoyment. And there and then, I tumbled into love."

"I saw no tumble," Alicia teased, not sure how she should respond to such a declaration. If she was honest, her tumble was delayed until he darted around a palm and coaxed her to waltz.

The Regent stood. The room fell silent. "Before we start dinner, we want to acknowledge the courage of someone who our dear friend, Sir Michael Anderton, and I have longed to recognise this past year. He now agrees for this story to be told." The Regent continued, mischief sparkling on his chubby face. "Matters of his heart allow the story of his remarkable bravery to be revealed."

Rochford shifted in his seat. Alicia suspected a growing discomfort.

The Prince rested a hand on Martin's shoulder. "I've been told you consider Viscount Rochford a coward due to his unexplained absence during a charge by the Horse Guards."

Martin did not stammer in his reply. "I do, yes. His absence occurred at a pivotal point in the battle. He was an officer, and he shirked his duty."

The Regent smiled at Martin, then across to Rochford, whose expression remained tranquil on hearing the accusations.

"You are incorrect, Marchant. Rochford saw our friend Anderton trapped beneath his horse, with no way of escape and the French soldiers moving to capture him." He shook his head, his distress obvious. "Or worse. Execution."

Ripples of conversation flowed around the table. Fans flicked open. Wine was consumed. Martin looked less confident, and Alicia cherished her growing sense of hope.

The Regent continued. "Risking his life, he fought through French soldiers to pull our friend to safety and ensure his survival." The Regent asked Martin, "Why am I permitted to tell this story now?" He looked down towards Rochford. "He wanted no recognition for his bravery during a fierce battle." His gaze returned to her brother, who seemed decidedly unsettled on hearing this tale. "He's a man who wishes to court your sister with your blessing."

Martin stammered. The Regent pressed gently on his shoulder. "There is time enough to clear the air." He looked towards Alicia with yet another good-humoured smile. "I hear you enjoy ice cream, Miss Marchant?"

"How could one not like ice cream?" she responded merrily, hoping to ease the surrounding tension. She heard a soft laugh next to her.

"Then I'm delighted to inform you we'll be serving rose-flavoured ices tonight. We are told roses symbolise true love, and Rochford bullied me into having it served this evening." His tone was teasing and amused.

Servants swarmed into the room with platters and began to serve. Attention eventually drifted away from Alicia and Rochford.

Alicia laid down her cutlery, leaned slightly towards Rochford and whispered, "Why did you laugh when I answered the Regent?"

"Because my lovely Alicia, you were, as always, honest. It's what captured me from the first moment you announced you were the 1816 Season's most successful wallflower."

"Well, Daniel, after what has occurred here tonight, I can no longer claim the title."

Capturing her hand, he lifted it to his lips and tenderly placed a soft kiss on her fingers.

"This is true. What a pair we are. Neither interested in marriage and it all changed thanks to Gunter's Tea Rooms, ice cream and meeting a school friend in Berkeley Square," he whispered, his voice laced with humour. "Should we invite Mr Gunter to our wedding?"

"Perhaps you should ask me to marry you before invitations are dispatched."

7
PLUTO AND OTHER WANDERING OBJECTS

NICKI BURNS

I'm not coming.

Kerrie and I have decided to be together.

I'm sorry.

Evie stared at the text message. The ice cream carton she'd been popping into the freezer tumbled from her hand to the tile floor of the mountain cabin's tiny kitchen. She had brought the good ice cream. The expensive stuff with bits in. She'd had a sense she'd be needing it. But not because of this. She certainly hadn't predicted this. She rang Joel immediately. He'd been her boyfriend for almost a year. He couldn't fob her off with just a three-line text. But it rang out. The blinking coward! She texted back:

What the heck?! You won't even talk to me?!

His next message came through immediately:

I think it's for the best.

No hard feelings, okay?

No hard feelings? In the melted puddle of her thoughts, Evie tried to figure out just what her feelings were. First up was disbelief. Was that a hard feeling? Joel had begged her to come on this couple's holiday with him the week before Christmas. Begged her. She hadn't wanted to do this again. As she'd told Joel, the other couple they'd gone on a few weekend trips away with were really more his friends than hers. In fact, she didn't think Kerrie and Hakim even liked her. Kerrie was always making snide comments about how Evie's outfits were 'brave', which was just an insult dressed up like a compliment with a fake moustache and big glasses. And Hakim barely deigned to speak to her at all, clearly thinking it not worth his time or effort. Joel had loudly denied it. "Why on earth wouldn't they like you?" he'd demanded to know. She couldn't answer. How was she supposed to know? Sure, she thought she was a likable person, but people had not liked her before.

On a few occasions at work, for example, when she'd been getting a cuppa from the staffroom, she'd been on the receiving end of waspish comments like, "Why are you always smiling?" or "What's there to be so happy about?" Such comments suggested she was too clueless to know about things like natural disasters and childhood leukemia, like the light in her eyes was the sun shining through the back of her empty head. But she shrugged off such suggestions. Usually. She was a naturally cheerful person and she refused to make apologies for it. Joel had insisted everyone liked her and that this little pre-Christmas getaway was just what they needed — but now he wasn't coming and he'd got together with Kerrie? That was a hard one to swallow.

Next up on the feelings block had to be anger. That definitely counted as a hard feeling, right? Although, ironically, the emotion itself rolled through her quite easily — anger at Joel and Kerrie but also at herself. She allowed herself to be put in this position. She should have known better. The next feeling would have to be relie—

"Aaaargh!"

Evie screamed when she realised she wasn't alone. A man loomed in the doorway.

"Evie?" The deep voice that haunted her dreams sometimes rumbled through the room.

"Hakim?"

"What are you doing here?"

"What do you mean? I'm supposed to be here."

"But I thought... that is, I was under the impression I would be the only one here."

"Were you? Because I was under the impression the four of us were spending the week here together."

Hakim peered around, his expression tense. "Is Joel here?"

"No. Just me," Evie replied.

Hakim's face relaxed. Evie narrowed her eyes at him.

"You knew he wasn't coming?"

Hakim nodded warily.

"And you know why?"

Hakim nodded again in a cautious way that set her teeth on edge.

"Yes, I know Joel and Kerrie—"

"I see." Evie cut him off. The tongue-tied effect he usually had on her seemed to have been swept away by the tide of humiliation of her current situation.

Hmph. A thin silver lining.

Evie shoved her phone into the pocket of her jeans, snatched up the ice cream tub off the floor and stomped over to the cutlery drawer to grab out some spoons. Then she slammed the drawer shut with a bang. Hakim winced.

"So everybody knew but me — silly old Evie, too stupid to see what was right in front of her face."

A strange expression passed across Hakim's face. If she had to put a name to it she'd call it 'despairing'. That had to be one of the hard feelings, didn't it? But she wouldn't have thought cool, collected Hakim would ever stoop to so messy an emotion. She must have imagined it. Still. He had been dumped just like she had. She supposed that warranted some solidarity. He might not be a nice person, but she was. She offered him a spoon of his own. He raised a sardonic eyebrow in response.

"Ice cream before dinner?"

She shook her head. "Ice cream for dinner."

"Ah." The Eyebrow of Judgement rose even further, disappearing under the black fringe that flopped across his golden forehead. "Even better."

"Are you ever not sarcastic? Is it really such a crime to care about things?"

The despairing expression flashed across his face again. Confusing man.

Hakim threw his hands up. "Zut alors! Je suis un imbecile."

Evie knew he spoke French, but she'd never heard him do so before. Swoon! No, wait. What was she thinking? No swooning. Bad Evie. On their first trip away together as a group of four Kerrie had told her that Hakim's family had immigrated from Algeria to Australia when he was thirteen. "That's why he's so exotic-looking," she'd giggled. Evie didn't much like that description. It made the assumption that white was the norm, which was ridiculous in a country as multicultural as modern Australia and even more ridiculous when remembering they all lived and worked on unceded Aboriginal land. More than half the kids in Evie's class weren't white.

"He's an astronomer," Kerrie had told her. "But remember that's different to an astrologer, so don't ask him about your horoscope." She'd smiled condescendingly and Evie had resisted the urge to grab the other woman by the shoulders and scream in her face, "I'm a teacher! I know what an astronomer is!"

So, no, on meeting Hakim she wouldn't have used the term 'exotic', but she would have used 'gorgeous' and 'regal'. If he'd suddenly decided to don a crown and a long velvet robe, people would assume he was some sort of dignitary, a VIP, rather than wondering if he was dressed up for Halloween. Evie, on the other hand, got asked if she was on her way to a fancy-dress party while wearing her everyday clothes. While she knew she brought that on herself with her love of bright colours and all things sparkly, she'd prefer to be able to wear what she liked without always having to hear other people's opinions on it.

Evie took her ice cream out to the lounge room and flopped onto the couch. Hakim followed, eyeing her warily, like one might an unexploded bomb. The windows were floor to ceiling and the view over the valley was truly spectacular. Hakim pointed out the window. "When the sun sets, we'll be able to see Venus dawning right there." Then he turned to her, concerned. "Is that mansplaining?"

Now it was Evie's turn to quirk an eyebrow, surprised he would know or care about such a concept.

"No, that would be if you started lecturing me on the most appropriate way to teach five-year-olds."

"Why would I do such a thing?"

"Well, you might do it if you assumed that as a man your uninformed opinion carried greater weight than a woman's expertise and experience."

"I know nothing about teaching or caring for little ones." Hakim shook his head. "But one day I hope to learn."

He watched Evie closely, as though her reaction to this statement was somehow important. Evie cleared her throat nervously, refusing to read too much into it, trying to keep the secret hopes she'd been quashing for months from rising to the surface. She and Hakim didn't discuss personal things like having children someday. They barely even shared smiles with each other.

The four of them had competed together in a pub quiz once and, in answer to the question "How many planets are there in the solar system?", Evie had immediately answered eight. Joel and Kerrie had laughed at her and insisted it was nine, practically patting her on the head. Hakim had interjected: "Evie is correct." Her foolish heart had fluttered madly. She had been shocked his mouth could actually form those words, let alone say them aloud. She was certain they all thought it was a lucky guess on her part.

"How long have you known?" Evie asked.

Hakim didn't insult her by pretending not to know what she meant.

"That Kerrie and Joel are sleeping together? A while."

Evie flinched as though slapped. "They've been sleeping together for a while? This didn't just happen?"

Hakim gave her a sidelong look and Evie flushed.

"I guess you think I'm pretty dumb. I happen to know that Pluto got downgraded from planet status in 2006 to possible dwarf planet status or "Look, we're just not really sure what it is" status, okay?" The trivia night had been a while ago, but she was clearly still holding a grudge.

"Of course you do," Hakim responded calmly, as though she hadn't just thrown a weird accusation at him out of nowhere. "You're a teacher." He said it so matter-of-factly, so without question, that for a moment Evie was too stunned to respond. Then, when she did, it was as though the floodgates opened and all the words came streaming out.

"It's interesting how many people on hearing I'm a kindergarten teacher suddenly assume I have the same mental capacity as the kids I teach. Sorry, did I say 'interesting'? I meant really annoying. Okay, so I've trained myself out of using real swear words and, yes, I am extremely familiar with all the escapades of Bluey and Bingo and, sure, I know all the Wiggles songs, but that doesn't mean I can't discuss serious topics as well. Liking the colour yellow doesn't mean I have the attention span of a toddler. For example, I despise using the term 'domestic violence' to describe men's violence against women and children. It reminds me of a sleight-of-hand magic trick by a sinister stage magician. Who is to blame? Wave the wand, say the magic word 'domestic', pull pack the curtain and — poof! — there's no-one there."

Hakim's eyes widened.

"Have I infantilised you? Was I hurtful?"

He looked so mortified that Evie's first instinct was to tell him, no, of course he hadn't hurt her feelings or made her cry in secret. That she longed for his good opinion wasn't his fault. But there had already been too much lying.

"More like brusque and dismissive."

He dragged his fingers down his face, groaning in what sounded like physical pain.

"I was aiming for polite but distant. I guess I" — he made the motion of a steering wheel — "overcorrected?"

"But why not just be friendly?" Evie winced a little at the whine in her voice, the hurt so obvious.

He ran his hand through his hair, mussing it all up, as he lay his head back on the couch and closed his eyes. "You weren't so friendly either."

"What?" Evie bristled.

"You wouldn't even give me a second glance."

"Well, of course not. I only ever saw you when I was with my boyfriend. I could barely give you a first glance, and that was hard enough."

Hakim sat up straight, eyes snapping open.

"What does that mean?" he asked urgently.

"Well, you know…"

"Faster. Explain faster."

"You're intelligent, gorgeous, well-read, fascinating." He stared at her as she rattled off his positive qualities. "I thought you were the complete package, really, except for already having a girlfriend and not being a very nice person, which is a deal-breaker, of course."

Hakim sighed, a deep, long-suffering sound that seemed to travel from his boots all the way up through his body.

"I avoided being too friendly because I thought you were—"

"A bimbo?"

"No!" He sounded shocked at the term, as though Evie, a young blonde woman with D-cup boobs, hadn't heard the term applied to her literally hundreds of times in her life.

"An airhead?"

"No," he said again, sternly this time, his eyebrows drawing down in a harsh 'V' shape.

"A ditz?"

"Lovely," he interrupted her. That stopped Evie in her tracks. She hadn't been expecting that. But he wasn't done.

"Heartbreakingly, overwhelmingly, life-alteringly lovely."

Evie's jaw dropped. She could feel herself gaping like a goldfish. A lovely one, apparently.

"But Kerrie—"

"Kerrie and I broke up several months ago, after the first trip the four of us took."

"And then you got back together."

"No."

Evie shook her head. "I'm not following. That first trip was almost a year ago. We all went away together only two months ago, and there were other trips in between. Why would you go on a couple's holiday with a woman you weren't in a couple with?"

"A stupid, deceitful thing to do." Hakim waved his arm around wildly. "For Kerrie, she wanted time to convince Joel she was the right choice for him and, for me, it was an exercise in torture, really."

"I don't know what that means."

He stared at her for a long moment. "Do you not? Can you really not know?"

Her yearning heart beat a little faster.

"It meant I got to see you, honey. It was the only way I got to see you."

Oh.

Silence fell between them.

"I broke up with Joel after our last trip," Evie said suddenly.

"You did?"

Evie nodded.

Hakim held her gaze.

"Why?"

"He didn't make my heart race. It didn't make me smile just knowing I was going to see him. It wasn't right being in a relationship with him when I didn't feel those things for him."

"But you feel them for someone else?"

"He wouldn't let go," Evie said, dodging the question. "He kept ringing me every day, pleading with me to give him another chance. That's why none of this makes any sense. I only came here because he begged me to."

"You agreed to get back together?"

"No." Evie was emphatic. "I thought I could use this trip to convince him we weren't right together so he could move on. Why didn't he just get together with Kerrie then?"

"He didn't want to lose you. I think he was stringing Kerrie along so she wouldn't tell you that he cheated. But I suppose she finally convinced him to pick her."

"You're saying he was sleeping with another woman in order to keep me? This is a lot to take in." Evie was suddenly having to view her relationship with not just one but three people through an entirely different lens. She sighed. "All four of us have behaved ridiculously, haven't we?"

Hakim stood then and drew Evie to her feet, placing his hands on her shoulders.

"You didn't answer my question before. Do you have feelings for someone else?" He leaned down so his breath was hot against her ear. He ran his fingers down the sides of her arms.

She shivered under his touch. It was suddenly quite difficult to remember how to breathe.

"Do you, Evie?" he whispered.

She nodded, her cheek brushing against his. He pulled her into an embrace and she hoped he'd never let go.

ⳍⳡⳍ

"Should we leave?" Hakim asked the next morning. They had fallen asleep together on the couch, cuddling and whispering sweet nothings to each other, eating ice cream and spilling secrets, but things didn't progress beyond that.

"No." Evie was emphatic. "This is our holiday. If we had come here together in the first place, what's something fun you'd have wanted to do?"

Hakim's eyes grew heated and, with a jolt of excitement, Evie realised his mind had turned to, well, *indoor* fun. That hadn't actually been what she'd meant, but she nevertheless felt a responding flash of interest. But she'd only just got out of a relationship yesterday. Sort of. She couldn't just leap straight into the arms of another man. Could she? Then Hakim smiled at her, a smile that warmed her right through to her bones, and she reconsidered.

But instead of suggesting they move to the bedroom, he said, "How about we go down to the village for brunch? Man cannot live on ice cream alone." He grinned. Evie felt equal parts disappointment and relief at the suggestion.

"Maybe man can't, but I think woman can," she rejoindered playfully.

"Ah," he leaned over and tweaked her nose in such an easy gesture of affection her heart squeezed in her chest. "But even the Cookie Monster had to diversify his diet."

They walked down to the village, chatting the whole way. Would climate change really make the planet unliveable by 2050? They talked about black holes and the expanding universe. But expanding into what? They gorged themselves on bacon and eggs and avocado toast at a cute little café.

Then Evie convinced Hakim to join her in feeding some alpacas at a nearby farm. They laughed until they cried when one sneezed all over him. After a long tramping bush walk, they made their way back to the cabin and curled up on the couch to watch *Die Hard*, objectively the best Christmas movie, they both agreed. When the credits rolled, he murmured into her ear, "And what now, mon amour, my darling girl?" He kissed her neck and she nibbled at his jaw. All the ice cream was gone, but that was okay. They had both found something better.

8
SAM'S SECRET
CLARE MILES

Josie gripped her mixing bowl like a lifeline, sorely craving the peace ice-cream making always brought. Yet it wasn't working any better tonight than it had for the past week. The freezers, jam-packed with her home-made pistachio ice cream, were testament to that. Instead, her mind remained trapped on a scene that she couldn't whisk, mix or beat her way past.

"Your Majesty," a gravelly voice she'd know anywhere, said behind her.

Her heart flipped despite having prepared herself for this moment. She'd known he would come back; his moral code wouldn't allow for anything less.

Slowly she turned, bowl clasped in both hands. Samson Winter stood two steps inside the closed kitchen door. Black jeans, t-shirt and leather jacket covered his don't-mess-with-me build, replacing his usual suit. She gulped and continued her inspection up past lips that held no hint of his hard-won smile, to eyes, dark and troubled.

Realising how utterly futile it had been to try and prepare for this, for him, she moistened suddenly dry pistachio-flavoured lips.

"You're back?" She hadn't meant to make it a question — it was a statement, a fact. Except her voice, a smidgen high, obliviated years of training. *Don't ever reveal your feelings.* Gut-churning, sleep-stealing feelings that tortured and tempted in equal measure.

His midnight blue eyes scanned every of inch of her. Starting at her bare feet, up past well-worn jeans, vintage apron, her mother's pearls, to a messy ponytail and face scrubbed clean of make-up. Her breath hitched and body quivered as flames of awareness followed his path. She was used to being inspected, analysed — it had happened every day of her life, would always happen. But never with this reaction. His gaze lingered on her lips for a heartbeat, for two, before landing on her cheek, where a hint of a bruise remained. Fury, then concern, flashed across his face, before his well-worn impassive mask fell into place.

He bowed his head in deferment, in acknowledgement.

"To resign." His low rumble filled the room.

She'd also expected this. Why then, did she clutch the bowl to her chest trying to ease the ache that lodged there?

"Why?" she asked, throwing a lifetime of caution to the wind. Yet the reality was she'd done that a week ago.

"You know why."

"I want you to say it. We need to be clear." Her thumping heart almost drowned out her own words.

"I crossed a line that I had no right to. I kissed you," he said in a no-argument-to-be-had tone.

It wasn't just a kiss. It was *The Kiss* that changed her life, changed her. No matter what happened, that fact remained.

"Technically, you kissed me back. And don't forget I crossed that same line."

"You were..." He planted his feet wider apart, clenched his fists. "...upset."

She made an unroyal-like snort.

"Furious, you mean. Don't sugar coat this and treat me with kid gloves."

He hadn't when he'd kissed her. She'd been jammed against his body, feeling hers leap alive. And for the first time in her life, she'd felt truly free. To be herself, a woman, not a queen.

"It's quite obvious I don't." His lips tightened. "And you had every right to be furious. For what it's worth, I'm glad you broke your engagement and kicked," he dropped his voice to a snarl, "Alfred Lord Hammersley to the curb."

"Threw under the bus, according to him."

Her fingers went to her still-tender cheek where Alfred had hit her.

"He's lucky to be alive," Sam growled, tracking her movement.

She didn't disagree.

Her self-defence punch had caught Alfred off guard. Sam smashing open the door and catching him in a flying tackle had terrified him. Not to mention when it had taken three others to drag him off Alfred.

But with her, Sam had been so tender. Once the adrenaline had worn off and Alfred had been dealt with, her legs had turned to mush. Sam had sat her down, iced her cheek, talked through her body-shaking anger, and got her a bowl of her favourite caramel ice cream. And then, when she'd smashed through a lifetime of expectations and listened to her heart, she'd kissed him, and he'd kissed her right back.

She clutched the bowl tighter, trying to stop her incessant inner turmoil, because the ramifications were huge, for both of them. But the voice inside, asking *what she wanted,* that went against every one of her teachings, refused to be quiet.

She squared her shoulders, decision made.

"I'm glad you're back, Sam."

ೞ౮౪౫

Her words echoed through the room, inside his head and threatened to dislodge his hard-fought resolve. She'd always called him *Agent Winter,* never his first name. Not even the night they'd kissed. A kiss that'd sent him from the palace to the open roads. He'd ridden his motorbike for days until he trusted himself not to track down that bastard who'd dare touch her and finish what he'd started. But no matter how far, how fast he went, he couldn't extinguish the feel, the taste of her.

He dragged his gaze from her forest-green eyes in case she caught even a glimpse of his feelings. Instead, he focused on the kitchen bench behind her, a mess of equipment covering its surfaces. His throat burned, knowing she was upset, sad. Because making ice cream was what she did every time she was. When her parents had died, she'd come in here, every night for a year. She'd finish her last engagement, put on one of her frilly old-fashioned aprons, and hole herself up in here. Alone. Like she'd done when a former school friend had sold her story to the tabloids, when a politician had questioned her aptitude for the role. Whenever she hurt.

His stomach clenched at the thought he'd done that to her. *Don't kid yourself, Winter, none of this is about you.* Her future husband was of national importance, international interest, not him. It didn't stop him from being kiss-the-ground relieved she wasn't marrying that fucker, Lord Hammersley. Not that he could stomach the thought of her marrying anyone. Which was when he'd realised his feelings for her were as dangerous as an oil-slicked road. With the greatest of difficulty, he'd managed to control himself, until that night.

"Not for long. I came to apologise, to tidy things up and leave, for good." *But most importantly to make sure you're all right, to see you one last time in person.*

"Apologise? We're back to the kiss?" Her eyes narrowed.

His gaze flew to her lips. Soft yet firm, they'd fitted perfectly against his. His hands clenched tighter, trying to forget how absolutely right it'd felt, when it'd been so obviously wrong.

"It doesn't matter what we're back to. We kissed and for that" — *I'm forever grateful, forever haunted* — "I'm sincerely sorry. It's no longer appropriate for me to continue as your bodyguard." His words were stiff and stilted like he was reading from a script. The words he never thought he'd say to anyone, especially to the one person he'd never wanted to let down.

"No, it's not," she agreed, as he'd expected. Why then did his stomach drop like he'd fallen from the tallest palace steeple as the reality of the years, decades, ahead hit? A barren wasteland separated from the flame-haired, green-eyed, sleep-stealing woman he loved.

Inwardly he cringed. *Loved.* He hadn't even been intimate with her, been on a date, met her family or friends, other than as an employee. *Remember all that, Winter, you fuckwit.* Still, he craved her company, more than anything.

"Leaving." She frowned. "To go where?"

Some place where I don't see your photo every day. Where I can't get internet access so I don't spend all day tracking you like some kind of weirdo stalker.

"Overseas, to start my own security firm, Your Majesty." He needed to remind himself who she was and wrap this up. He'd resigned, apologised, seen with his own eyes she was okay. Now he should be heading back to his apartment, packing his things and getting out of here, for good. Instead, he remained where he was, every sense fixed on her.

"You called me Josie last week," she said in a soft, intimate voice he'd never heard before. The hairs at the back of his neck rose. He rubbed a rough hand over them and pushed his boots further into the tiles.

"I did a lot of things that weren't appropriate that night," he reminded them both.

"So you said, and you're *sincerely sorry* for kissing me." Twin spots of red sat bright on her pale cheeks. "Is that the same as regret?" She bit down on her lip but raised her chin to look straight into his eyes.

Never. The answer resounded through him, despite the ramifications, the fact that he should. Instead, one taste had unlocked something deep and dark within him that he struggled to hold. He'd learned never to want anything, other than to keep her safe. He no longer had that right, the best he could do was leave.

Except her eyes, brimming with vulnerability, hit him like a sledgehammer. He stiffened and heaved in a breath to ease the ache as her light floral scent wafted over him and filled his lungs until he knew she deserved the truth.

CRESO

Josie watched his chest expand and shoulders stiffen. She automatically braced herself, her heart pounding so loudly she was surprised he couldn't hear it.

"No." His lips barely moved.

It took a second for his response to hit. Her mouth opened in surprise as the tiniest wedge of hope squeezed its way in and lodged in her heart.

"Neither do I," she admitted with a tremor in her voice, clinging to her courage.

"Really?" His tone, dark and rough, ran down her spine like an ice cube on a summer's day.

He smiled. A rare, beautiful tilting of full lips and a flash of white teeth. *I want to see more of that smile. More of him.*

She gulped and nodded.

"But it can't happen again." His lips flattened.

"Why, was it bad?" It certainly hadn't been for her. "Or you're not interested in me... in that way?" she ended in a horrified whisper. Had she totally misjudged this? Had this... tug towards him, that she'd fought for years, been completely one-sided?

He stepped towards her, a study of lethal grace.

"Oh, I'm interested in you... in every way." His husky voice prickled her skin and slammed her heart against her ribs. "So much that I've broken the code I've lived by, that gave my life meaning. You see, I've fallen for you, in every way possible."

Relief threatened to turn her to jelly as she put the bowl on the bench. Hiding the tell-tale shake in her legs, she took a step towards him.

"Do you know why Alfred was chosen for me at birth?"

What the hell?

He'd just laid his heart, guts, and everything else on the line and she mentioned *him, that dick.*

"I assume because he comes from one of the oldest, wealthiest, most influential families in the country, a powerful alliance by your side." *Everything I'm not.*

"Yes that, but also one of the most decent, most respected families. My father thought that would ensure I'd have someone I could trust by my side. He knew I'd need that, more than anything. And the thing is, Sam," she ran her fingers over her never-without mother's pearls, "I trust you. Completely."

Blood roared through his ears and he ran a desperate hand over his hair, fighting to keep himself together.

"My job's always been to protect you, take a bullet for you, which I'd willingly do. I broke that trust." He didn't even try to hide his anguish.

"You didn't. You changed it, for which I'm forever grateful. You see, I've wondered, for far longer than good for my sanity, what it would be like... with you." She speared him with a look that squeezed his heart. "And the last thing I'd *ever* want is for you to be harmed in any way. That" — she pinned him with a look of pure horror— "I couldn't live with."

Her words surged through him and almost buckled his legs.

"Josie." He took a moment to savour the sound of it on his lips. "You have the blood of your royal ancestors flowing through you. I have the blood—" he swallowed past the boulder in his throat "—of a murderer." What he'd worked his whole life to... overcome. He took a step back although every instinct screamed to move towards her. "You've read my dossier. You know my father killed my mother. This," he pointed between them, "can't go anywhere. You deserve better than that. Than me."

"Your father, Sam, not you. Never you." She stepped forward and took his hands in hers. Her small capable hands completely oversized by his, simultaneously unsettling and anchoring him. "I don't need to read your dossier to know you." She raised wonder-filled eyes to him. "You play basketball for relaxation, for sport. You organise matches between the bodyguards, and you hate to lose. But you wouldn't cheat, nor are you a bad loser. I know you play at the local boys' home, spending countless hours teaching, mentoring, hanging out with them." His sharp intake revealed his surprise. "Ha. You're not the only one with sources."

She winked, such an un-Josie-like thing to do, laughter burst from him.

"Let's see, what else?" She squeezed his hands. "Well, I'm not going to deny that I find you easy on the eye, you'd own a mirror after all." He felt heat scorch up his cheeks. "And I can make you blush. That could be interesting." She gave him a smile full of promise. "Pistachio ice cream is your favourite food, which is why there's a mass of it hogging the freezers, much to the despair of Chef." Her voice lowered, all jest disappearing. "You're loyal and steadfast and my favourite person, in this big crazy world, to spend time with."

Her sincerity smashed through every self-protection barrier he had. His eyes smarted, and for one horrified moment he thought he'd cry.

He swallowed.

"Josie." He rasped the name he'd never tire of saying. Raising a far from steady hand he ran a forefinger gently down her cheek and cupped her chin. "What are you asking for? Something casual?" He shivered, knowing he couldn't stomach anything less than permanent, and called on all his courage to tell her why. "I need more than that. Because—" He paused before telling her what he'd never told another. "I love you."

CRS80

"You love me?" she whispered, not daring to believe her ears.

He nodded, his expression raw and vulnerable, so unlike the man who veiled his feelings for a living.

"That's a relief, because I love you, so very much."

"You do?"

His eyes darkened to almost black and burned into hers.

She smiled, nodded and laughed all at once.

"And I don't want casual either. I get why you'd want to start your firm elsewhere. I'll come visit you as often as I can. I'll call, message, video, everything, anything."

"You'd do that? For me?" he asked, low and unsteady.

"Without question."

He dropped his hands to her waist and tugged her closer, enveloping her in his hot spicy scent, which she'd crave to her dying day.

"Once the press get a whiff of this..."

"You're embarrassed of me?"

He huffed out a laugh.

"Never." His expression turned serious. "But they'll have a field day, and the Establishment—" he shook his head "—won't ever forgive you."

"I can live with that. You know better than anyone what my life's like. The lack of privacy, spontaneity. The endless duties and speculation. But, Samson Winter." She anchored her hands on his shoulders. "I never knew I could feel this way.

That's why I broke my engagement. I couldn't, no matter the promises made in my name, marry him. You see there's been this dark-haired, six-foot-three impediment taking up my heart." His racing pulse and short ragged breaths matched hers. "But I don't want you to feel obligated." Her lips trembled. "I've wrestled with this. It's the most selfish thing I've ever done. Don't think I don't know what I'm asking of you."

"Hey, hey. There are many things I feel for you, obligation's nowhere on the list." He took one of her hands and placed it over his heart. "I feel you here. With every beat."

His heart pounded beneath her palm, sound and true, like him.

"I'm under no illusion that parts of it," he lowered his voice to a delicious rumble, "won't be a joyride. But you, Josephine Margaretta Elizabeth Sophia Sutton-Richmond, are entirely worth every stuffy courtier, tedious protocol, dirt-bag paparazzi, duty-filled day."

Her fingers gripped his cotton t-shirt and she struggled not to cry.

"I know you can't ever leave, that this is your life forever. That's why I'm going to start my firm here." He pushed back the lock of hair that had escaped her ponytail. "I don't want anything to separate us. I'm giving us every chance."

"And just when I think you couldn't be more perfect." She blinked away the tears that threatened.

"You think I'm perfect?" His slow sexy smile tumbled her insides. "There'll be plenty of times I'll happily remind you of that. Not now though, now I'm busy."

Slowly he lowered his head, his lips meetings hers. Suddenly he pulled back and scooped her into his arms in one quick manoeuvre.

Her squeal echoed around the room. "What are you doing?"

"Spontaneity won't ever be a problem." He grinned down at her while grabbing a tub of ice cream from the freezer, a devilish light in his eyes. "And ice cream, we're going to use lots of it."

9
SOFT SERVE AND COMFORT

VICTORIA BROWN

I t starts with a glance. A fleeting connection. How clever are eyes. What they absorb in that nano-second. His, the pale blue of a summer sky. Even better, they're perfectly spaced apart. Such a silly fetish of mine. Neat light-brown hair, olive complexion and fashioned stubble on a squared jaw. *Hot!*

But it's also the downside to eyes. Mine spy the soft-serve about to meet his lips. A feeling stirs in my gut, and not from any lactose intolerance. Anxious worms hatch and writhe, shooting a sickening wave of emotions to the surface.

I look to my dog Rusty who's busy sniffing the sidewalk smorgasbord — his tail a happy waving aerial as he scuttles in arcs. I tug his lead and flee.

Reading the letter that afternoon had split my heart into a million pieces. Desperate to be anywhere but the house, I'd found myself at the park, two blocks away.

And now? I'm retreating and out of breath. Back to my refuge.

Next day after work, I play ten games of phone solitaire and check my watch twenty times, battling the compulsion to walk. I'm an idiot. A desperate one, who's read one too many romance novels and imagined the connection. However, I simply can't ignore the niggle that he might be there again. Yesterday's liaison had sparked something beautiful in my troubled soul. Best antidote ever to the letter's horror. A final check. 4.30 pm. I shake the leash. "Come on, Rusty."

He spins and barks.

My heart dances as we near the bench. He's there. Perfectly sculptured lips widen in a smile. *Yeaahhh! I didn't imagine it!* Cute dimples appear, making him more deliciously handsome. I discreetly return the greeting, indulging in a quick facial study. Medium nose, full cheeks, broad forehead. Honest and kind as well as scorching hot, I conclude.

But damn! He's holding another sickening soft-serve. A dot of it graces the edge of his mouth. My silly fingers itch to wipe it, sparking that horrible wormy reaction. I swallow, watching him graduate to a creamy grin and a "Hello" that's deep, sexy and welcoming. Every bone in my body is pleading to stop. Tingles run down my spine. *Am I game?*

At my miniscule hesitation, Rusty parks his furry bottom. And eyes the ghastly treat, licking his chops. *Conspirator!*

Mine fall on it too. Stomach lurches.

"Hi," is all I manage.

Rusty shoots me a disapproving glare as I drag him, backside and all, along the path.

CGED

Next day, Saturday, I'm pacing the house. I've avoided the washing and cleaning — not hard to do. Too busy watching the clock and begging the clouds outside to stave off dumping their contents. 4.30 pm finally arrives and having become deeply invested in my romantic nonsense, Rusty's furry lips grin at me — I swear — as I clip the rope to his collar. My heart matches the pace of his legs. And like a guided missile, my eyes home in on Mr Amazing seated at the other end of the park. I mentally fist pump and head toward him.

"Hullo again." A broad grin this time.

Oh My God! Flawlessly shaped and crystal-white teeth.

"Have you got time to sit?" Lick. Lick. Lick.

A protest rises from deep within. To halt the panic, I force my gaze to his hand gesture. *You can do this.*

Rusty helps by gluing his bum to the pavement with eyes fixated on the creamy cone.

I'm too close. The sickly-sweet smell hits my nostrils. Spawning larvae brew within. *Go away!* I order my shoulders to fashion a shrug.

"Oh. Why not."

And proudly park my butt. *Thank you head for shoving my anxiety to the naughty corner.*

"What sort of dog is he?"

"Miniature Irish Wolfhound."

He hesitates. "Um. Aren't they grey? Not tan. Actually... er... do mini ones exist?"

"They do now."

We both giggle.

A warmth runs through me. My heart plumps up.

Rusty shoves a proud nose in the air, clearly aware he's the topic of conversation.

"He's confirming his status on pseudo-wolfhoundness," I add.

His extra toothy laugh melts me. Almost as much as the offensive creamy item in his hand.

"Hi... at last. I'm Cody Chambers."

"Jess Borden."

"And what do you do, Jess?"

"I'm an accounts clerk for Simmons. And you?"

"Mechanical fitter for Graded Transport."

No wonder the bod's so tight.

Wow! We've managed thirteen sentences in the presence of the cone without me throwing up. He seems embarrassed about eating in front of me. *You lovely, well-mannered man.* Thank goodness licked items aren't for sharing. Nevertheless, my stomach's plotting a take-over from the earlier head control. Swallowing profusely, I look away, tasting bile.

"Better go. Nice chatting."

My legs leap into action and Rusty glares as I drag him.

Thirteen whole sentences? Friggin' hopeless.

I scurry along, agonising over the cruel irony. What is your message, universe? Are you sending me a move-on order? Is he an axe murderer? Rapist? Or simply that it's time to bury this soft-serve gremlin. My tummy lurches and head whirrs at the thought, like a volcano about to erupt. My hormones argue their case, because Cody's certainly off the Richter scale.

◌♥◌

The next day, he's here again. But nooo! He's holding *two* of them. This can't be happening. Can I pretend not to see him?

Rusty train-engine yanks me to the bench and promptly stops.

"Hi."

"Hullo again. Is that for me? Thank you."

Cody's kind, sweet smile liquifies me more than the offering in his hand as I sit. I politely take it. *What on earth do I do now?*

The extended delicacy hovers one second too long, proffering Rusty a mixed message. It's gone in seconds.

Our eyes lock in a what-just-happened moment.

"Sorry. He was... um... a street dog in a past life."

Cody chuckles.

I laugh. I even relax. Those eyes. Delicious lips. Extended muscular legs. Who wouldn't?

"Take mine? I haven't started it yet."

He shoves it in front of my nose.

Help! The creaminess, sweetness, vanillaryness. *Please brain. Please gut. Please body. Be kind.* Too late.

"No thanks. Gotta go."

I dash yet again to the safe haven of home and give Rusty a pat.

"Thanks mate, but why didn't you snatch both?"

I'm seething now. The universe is telling me to let it go. Why else would it deliver Mr Sweet Super Hunk with a soft-serve added?

CR80

I plonk next to him the following day. Next to his ice cream and next to the one he's bought for me. *Again.* How kind. I'm trying to ignore it.

He must pick up on my demeanour — wriggling, shuffling feet and staring out to the park — because he calmly says, "I thought maybe you didn't like plain, so I had sprinkles added."

"That's lovely. Thank you." I take the offering.

Rusty barks.

"I think he prefers choc-dipped." Cody adds with a grin.

I try to enjoy the joke as I gulp away the stomach onslaught.

Then my stupid eyes land on what's in my grasp and they unkindly pool with backed-up tears. *Noooo. Not phase two!* Gut wrenching phase one is hard enough. I turn away, hoping he hasn't noticed, edging the offending item to my side.

In an instant, it's demolished.

"Rusty! You naughty boy."

My tone prompts dog-guilty response — ears flattened, nose dropped, eyes up.

I'll apologise later.

"Geez, he's quick."

I fake-giggle. "Maybe I need to feed him once in a while."

Cody chuckles.

My gut and heart settle, despite one offending item still in my midst. It's far enough away. Crisis averted.

Then Rusty paints an apologetic line of white residue down my leg with his coated tongue. I spy it. I smell it. Phase-two flood gates beg to open. Once they do, it'll be a friggin' three-tissue-box spillway.

I look away, white-knuckle gripping Rusty's lead. "I just remembered I left the oven on. Bye."

Collapsing through the door, the three-tissue-box howl materialises. Rusty nestles in. I sink my face into his wiry fur.

"Sorry for telling you off. I'm such a bad mother."

I'm *really* angry now. All I've managed to share with Cody is our names and work status. "We're more a business arrangement than potential..." I can't finish the sentence.

❧

In the morning I pace the corridor, cursing. It becomes a waste of a Sunday. 4.30 pm arrives. Do I go? I've made such an arse of myself he probably won't be there. But a little niggle, a tiny, finch-like peck nags at my heart. A friggin' angry crow jabs at my lower region.

I drag on my brave pants. Clouds are building as I poke my head out the door. A wily wind, cold and uninviting, is whipping about. *Forget it, universe. I'm not giving up.* I pull on a jacket and grab an umbrella. Off we go.

But the bench is empty. Of course, it would be. Silly, silly girl. Who'd want to be with a runaway, bleeding heart, high maintenance, emotional princess like me? Not that he's had a chance to discover *all* that yet.

The next day, the same. And the next.

In desperation, I drive past his work. Which is stupid because I don't know his car. I Face-stalk. He rarely posts, but has so many friends I ditch the axe-murderer/rapist theory. Twitter, Tinder, Instagram. I've now scored honours in Predator 101.

A week goes by. Each time we walk, Rusty looks up at me asking permission to sit at the empty bench. The tug on the leash answers him. The tug at my heart answers me. "Give up, you star-crossed lover!" Only, I can't.

After another week, the universe orders me to abandon my mission with a clap of thunder. I try, but still fail to heed it. Off I go regardless. "There's always tomorrow," I chant to it in hope. Only, that never comes, does it? If nothing else, Rusty and I are getting fit. Sadly though, my Cody liaison is now as fleeting as that first glance.

മ്പ

Sunday afternoon, under a sprinkling of rain, I venture out and gasp. *He's there.*

My excited-little-girl heart does a flip. My feet Irish jig. Rusty performs his own version, adding three pirouettes. I untangle him.

"Hullo," I manage, in pixie voice. I clear my throat. And glare at the cone. *How dare you try to ruin things.*

"Oh Jess. I'm so glad you came. I thought I'd never see you again. I had to fly to a mine out bush for an emergency breakdown."

A size-100 sigh escapes and I'm suddenly all girlish grins as we exchange numbers. Despite the vanilla mass poised at his mouth, I bravely ogle his waiting tongue. It's pink and broad and inviting... My insides simmer — in a good way, for a change. I'm feeling proud at having graduated one baby step from flight-and-fright-soft-serve school. This is the best day.

Then the offensive item slips near Cody's thigh while he's busy talking and is gone in a millisecond.

Very thoughtful, my precision cone-thief. "Naughty boy, Rusty!"

We laugh. We chat. With flirtatious looks and squirming added. Definitely the best day.

Then Cody frowns, rubbing his hands between his extended thighs and hesitates for what feels like forever before asking, "Why were you sad the other day? Why do you run? Um... What prick broke your heart, Jess?"

My throat jams. "Er. No prick. It's... not like that." How do I explain that soft-serve sets me off? He'll want to have me committed.

"Well... Whoever... I hate to see you so torn up."

I swallow. My throat doesn't clear. My insides turn to a river of molten lava and try to erupt. I stand to leave.

Only this time, a firm hand grabs me. And, like a miracle, his caring grip has a domino effect. My arm tingles, shooting electric sparks to every nook and cranny of my body. I plonk on the bench and grind my feet into the ground as Cody releases me. *Shame.* But two baby steps in one day? *Woo hoo.* The thought frees my voice. "The stupid sink in the bathroom decided to block up this morning."

Cody shakes his head with pursed lips, clearly acknowledging my change of subject, but doesn't pursue the matter — politeness gold.

"I could take a look at it. Do you live nearby?" His cheeks redden. "Of course you do."

We both chuckle.

"It's ok. I googled how to fix it."

"Ooooh?" His lips pout in a playful sulk.

Repair plumbing? My office hands beg to be excused from the task. And my revved-up body screams for more of him.

"Well... if you insist."

Thank goodness I'd forced myself to clean instead of wallowing in Cody-self-pity today.

He leaps from the bench. "Let's go."

Rusty bounds into action and proudly leads the way — tail high, with staccato-prancing legs and a smug expression on his furry face.

We chat and grin, all flirty-like.

I'm zinging more with every step, my hand begging to find his.

Arriving home, I open the front door.

"Ok. Where's this offending basin?"

"Through here."

I lead him to the bathroom.

He opens the cupboard below it and peers in.

"Is this a rental? Because the pipework's pretty old."

"Um. No."

"Right then. Have you got any tools?"

"In the shed. I'll get the key."

Moments later, he comes waltzing into the kitchen, carrying a box and grinning.

"Look what I found!"

My mouth turns to a desert. All the blood leaves my body. I collapse into the nearest chair.

"Jess! Jess! What's wrong?"

"It's the..." My finger jabs in the direction of the repulsive object. "I'm sorry."

Cody dumps it on the kitchen bench and is instantly on bended knee next to me as a tear rolls down my cheek.

His fingertip gently whisks it away.

"No need for sorry. Was it *the ice-creams* that made you run? Was this your... boyfriend's soft-serve machine?"

"No. Oh no. It was my grandmother's."

I sob, licking my parched lips and forcing air into my lungs.

"Nan always made me soft-serve. You see, she and Pop raised me. They were wonderful."

"Oh?" His eyes are questioning as he stands.

I gulp. "My parents died in a car accident when I was four."

"Oh my God! That's so tragic. And now?"

"Pop died a couple of years ago. I'd moved out by then and visited Nan every Saturday. But, um..." Another swallow... "One day, I found her asleep. Permanently. I think she died of a broken heart."

His hand whips to his mouth to cover the gasp. "Oh Jess. You poor love. When?"

"A year ago."

Without speaking, he pulls me up to him. I fall into his warm chest, feeling his heart beat regular and steady. It slows mine. Muscular arms encircle me. Fingers caress the small of my back. His breath is whispery on my neck. It's too much. A tidal wave of grief hovers. I stiffen and move away.

"Tell me more." He releases me.

Swallow. Swallow. I've officially gulped more in the last few minutes than the last year.

"I had a great life. A good job, partner, friends, parties, sports, everything. But when Nan died, I fell in a hole. After weeks in bed, going to work was all I could manage. My partner didn't handle it, so I moved in here. He got the friends, sports and parties. I got Rusty."

"Jeez. That's really rough. Do you have any close relatives?"

"No."

"It must be hard living here with all the reminders and memories."

He sweeps a strand of hair from my cheek, which warms at the touch. I look up. His sky-blue eyes are bursting with tenderness and compassion.

"On the contrary: I needed it. I felt like she was kinda still here or at least looking after me from somewhere. It helped."

"Oh. I see."

"Then I got a letter saying it was mine. All of it. And suddenly... Nan was gone. Poof! Just like that."

The flood gates open. His arms envelop me. I burrow in. Warm hands rub my back. After a while I sniff and drag my head from his sodden t-shirt, swatting the area as if that might remove the stain. "Sorry."

"Don't be." With the tip of his forefinger he dabs at a last watery drop snaking its way down my cheek.

"When the letter arrived, I had to escape the house. I grabbed Rusty and fled to the park. And there you were. On the bench. You. And a damn soft-serve. I couldn't help it. I ran."

"What a klutz. I kept buying them to have an excuse to sit without looking like a pervert... or worse. Hoping *you'd* come along. From that first glance, I was hooked, Jess." He grins. "Probably gained a few kilos."

I laugh too, brimming with relief and gaze into his soft-blue eyes.

He deepens the intent with them and, in slow motion, coaxes my chin up with two fingers. My heart pounds as his lips press onto mine. They're moist and silky and teasing. The tip of his broad, hot tongue prises my mouth open. *Oh my God!* Heat surges through me as his kiss deepens. Our lips mould together and tongues explore. After quite a while, I edge away to come up for air.

The soft-serve ice-cream maker catches my eye.

Cody follows my line of sight and pulls me in close. "I'll get rid of it."

I study it, feeling no stomach lurch. Or impulse to cry. Just a wave of tranquillity and appreciation.

"No." I look up at Cody with a smile. "What flavour would you like? I'm having chocolate."

Rusty barks.

"You're not allowed chocolate," I scold.

We both laugh.

10

THE MOST BEAUTIFUL WOMAN

LUCY LEVER

S ara looks for Henry in the crowded, brightly-lit arrivals hall of Sydney International Airport, holding onto her bags and smiling at strangers in a bid to appear as confident and relaxed as a local. She checks her phone for messages. Nothing.

Where is he?

"I'm here," she texts, hesitates, then adds a smiling emoji. If she has to wait too much longer, she'll send him a sad face. Or a broken heart.

Keep it together, Sara. Henry will show up. He has to.

She finds a place to sit, puts her feet up on her bags, and watches the last passengers from her flight disappear, alone, or in the company of family or friends.

What if he doesn't come at all?

The doubt claws at her heart. She'll wait for him for no more than half an hour, and then she'll use her phone to find accommodation in some beachside suburb and jump into a taxi.

She'll buy a selfie stick and spend a month posting shots of herself in summery locations to convince her kids she's having a blast, and then she'll go home and cheerfully pick up where she left off.

Everything will be familiar. She might have to stay with one of her daughters until she can rent somewhere, but she'll have the same friends, the same family, the same life as before. She can work from anywhere. The madness of this journey across the world in search of middle-aged love a mere bump on the road to her comfortable twilight years.

"How was the Sydney trip?" her English friends will ask.

"Fabulous," she'll say. "The man never showed up, but boy did I get to see some great art/shops/food/beaches." She'll curate her experience for each friend depending on their interests.

And yet, it won't be the same. She's already spent half her life trying to get over damned Henry, and now she'll have to start all over again. The Australian bloody well shadowed her marriage, so the poor Englishman never had a chance.

"You can't compare an idealised relationship with a real one," the counsellor had said. But it was no good. That was exactly what she'd done, despite her best efforts. She and her husband had both hung in for the post A-levels divorce, seeing the last of their chickens off to university in Bristol before letting the axe fall on their marriage and their comfortable cottage on the outskirts of Bath.

If Henry lets her down, she'll be compelled to fill her spare time with energetic country walks in miserable weather, trips to the cinema, choir and book club. Or perhaps ice cream and whisky.

Seeking reassurance, she reaches into her handbag and carefully pulls out a yellowing piece of paper, the letters and numbers nearly faded away under long-dry splotches of vanilla and passionfruit ice cream. Holding it brings back a flood of memories.

❧

That scorching-hot summer day of her long-ago gap year when she'd walked straight off the beach into the crowded Manly ice cream shop for the first time. Damp towel wrapped around her bikini, wet hair, bare sandy feet — who knew hot bitumen could *burn* tender British feet?

The colourful array of flavours laid out before her almost as seductive as the man who waited for her order behind the counter. Henry had been dazzling at twenty, with his Australian tan, his shock of golden-brown hair, and his wicked smile. Not to mention the crisp white T-shirt that barely concealed his finely muscled surfer's body.

"What would you like?" he'd asked innocently enough.

"I'll have a vanilla cone, please," she said.

"Vanilla?" His eyes burned into hers.

"You could add a scoop of passionfruit." She wanted to share her ice cream with him, and perhaps a lovely cool shower...

He wrote his name and phone number on a piece of paper and slipped it into her hand along with her change...

❧

For their first date he took her on an adventure up and over wild cliffs, down a dirt track, and a ladder that was nothing more than a series of footholds carved one beneath the other into a sheer rockface, with a thin, frayed rope to hold onto when courage failed. He scaled down in seconds.

"You're going to be fine," he said. "Here, I'll help you work out where to put your feet."

"I've crossed the busiest intersections of London against the lights," she said with a bravado she didn't feel as he gently grasped her foot with a steady hand and guided her down.

He took her into his arms at the bottom of the ladder to still her shaking body, and their inevitable kiss was as delicious and delectable as the first mouthful of a thick, creamy hazelnut-caramel ice cream on a hot summer afternoon, times one thousand. No-one had *ever* kissed her like that.

Afterwards they swam languidly in the rockpools at the base of the cliff, marvelling at their flourishing underwater gardens, complete with giant snails and a single, shy blue-ringed octopus.

On their second date he taught her to surf. She managed to stay upright on the longboard on her tenth, or perhaps her twentieth attempt, riding a gentle wave into shore shouting, "I did it, I did it!" She let go of her board in the shallows as Henry picked her up and swung her around, laughing.

"You're amazing," he said, "as well as being the most beautiful woman in Manly."

Sara wasn't size ten, or even size twelve. She loved ice cream too much. But at that moment, years of subliminal and overt messages glorifying the rake-thin woman meant nothing compared to the look in his eyes. For the first time in her life she *felt* beautiful.

No wonder their farewell was so tough.

Sara was due to begin university and Henry had obligations to his work, the family ice cream business. They said their goodbyes at Sydney Airport.

They kissed again and again, oblivious to the stares of passers-by. He ran his fingers roughly through her hair. His voice was hoarse. Her face was wet with tears. It was as if she was off to war. She very nearly looked around for her fellow comrades in arms.

"Bye Henry," she said, pressing her body against his.

"We'll see each other again. I'll make sure of it." He wiped away her tears.

"Is that a promise?"

"It's a promise."

But his dad was sick for a long time before he passed away, and his mum needed support, and he couldn't get away from the business.

She was about to buy a plane ticket when her mum left her dad, and her dad fell apart and asked her to stay close, and the university invited her to continue on to a post-graduate degree, and by then she couldn't afford the flight...

Before they knew it they were married to other people and their lives had moved on.

The two of them lost touch. At least until he tracked her down online after his divorce, the renewed contact precipitating the crash and burn of her own marriage.

Perhaps he really was nothing but a happy dream. A figment of an imagination overwrought by watching and reading an excess of romance, usually accompanied by an ice cream. Or two.

ജ്ഞ

Sara opens an app on her phone, ready to search for accommodation. Her body is heavy with exhaustion. She yearns for a place to nap. In the bathroom mirror on the plane, bags under her bloodshot eyes had made her look older than her years, despite the new dress she'd bought in Chelsea.

"Very flattering," the young sales assistant had said of the dress, surreptitiously glancing at her pink digital watch. They were getting close to closing time.

"What do you mean, flattering?" Sara had asked.

"It makes you look... um, younger."

Sara wasn't convinced, but she'd bought the dress anyway, because she wanted to believe it possible that she *could* look younger. Now it feels way too tight and just wrong.

Perhaps it's best that he doesn't see her travel-stained like this.

But she looks up from her phone and he's there.

Her silver fox. Monsieur Gorgeous. Okay, his hair might be a little thinner, but his lines fall in all the right places, and he's still sexy and tanned and, well, hot. Piping hot. She forgets to be cranky that he's late, and she's preparing to launch herself into his arms, when something about his expression makes her change her mind.

Uh-oh. Cue shark music. The joy seeps out of her and her voice catches in her throat.

He holds himself stiffly. His smile is forced. Something's not right.

It's *her*.

It's the dress. Her hair. Her size. Her jetlagged state and obvious and urgent need for a shower. Her age — which, by the way, is still the same as his, so it's a bit rough if that's his problem.

They've been speaking on video apps for months, so surely he knew that at fifty-eight she no longer looks as she did at twenty. But online she'd always made sure she was wearing something fresh and stylish, with a little make-up, her bookshelves or some nice art the backdrop, as if for a conference call or job interview.

"Hi," he says now, without reaching out to touch her. "I'm so sorry. I was held up at work. And I left my phone at home by accident this morning. How was your flight?"

Her flight was a shocker if he really wanted to know. She'd been jammed in the middle row between two large men who not only snored but monopolised their shared arm rests. In front, a fretful baby, whose glamorous parents looked as terrible as she felt by the time they landed. Each of Sara's frequent trips to the toilet had required high-level diplomatic skills, as she squeezed past one or the other of her grumpy neighbours.

"The flight was great," she trills, wishing she felt relaxed enough to tell Henry the awful truth and laugh about it. "Just great."

"Let me help you with your bags," he says, scanning her loaded trolley. Can he not bear to look at her? Is his disappointment so acute? She could be on her way to her snug English bed right now, to sleep soundly, and then wake up to an ordinary winter's day in familiar surroundings, her regular morning routine; staggering bleary-eyed to her coffee machine, the BBC radio news, nobody to impress.

They say little in the car. He keeps his eyes on the road and she stares out the window as they crawl through the traffic, and under the harbour and through more traffic, until she recognises the winding road to Manly, to his new, spacious apartment overlooking the water. She'd anticipated this drive from the other side of the world, imagining the two of them laughing, chatting, touching occasionally, as he pointed out the city's landmarks. Unable to keep their hands off each other. The sexual tension building. As if they were a couple of teenagers. What *had* she been thinking?

The lift is out of order, so they drag her bags up three flights of stairs, stopping on each landing to catch their breath. So much luggage for what will now be a short stay.

Once they're inside, she snatches a moment to take in her surroundings. The living room is light-filled, with a work desk that was to be hers overlooking a break where wetsuit-clad surfers vie for the perfect position in readiness for the next wave. The intense blue of sky and sea hurts her tired eyes.

And yet his cool reserve has her still feeling immersed in the drab greys of the English winter she's left behind.

There's only one bedroom. They line up her bags next to the couch, as if in mutual agreement it will be her bed until she can book a flight home.

"It's a beautiful apartment," she says, looking at a cluster of photos of his children when they were small. She must not become attached to the place, to him, to his family, to her nebulous dream that they might marry one sunny day on a beach somewhere, her with her arms loaded with yellow wattle, him in a loose cotton shirt, white against his tanned skin.

"Yes. I love it here." He gazes out the window, at the light, the sky. "I know you're tired after the flight, but you should stay awake for the benefit of..." he searches for the right words, "your Circadian rhythms. So, perhaps a walk along the beach? Then we can go somewhere to eat."

"That's a brilliant idea." She feigns enthusiasm. She would prefer to sink into the couch, to sleep, to slip into temporary oblivion. Circadian rhythms be damned.

She takes fresh clothes into the bathroom with her to shower and change, avoiding the mirror.

The afternoon is wearing on, but the beach sand is still warm under their bare feet, the eddies of water deliciously cool. Children dig castles, families play beach volleyball, a couple practise capoeira on the promenade. Everyone seems happy. Sara resists the impulse to take Henry's arm.

"Isn't this great?" she asks.

"Yes it's wonderful," Henry says, his expression melancholy, his eyes downcast.

They eat an early dinner overlooking the water, watching the ferries making their way across the harbour as twilight falls. She fills the awkward silence by asking him about the health of his family members, one by one, as she struggles to keep her eyes open, hoping she doesn't doze off and drop face first into her meal.

"Let's go," he says, before dessert and in the midst of a laboured dissection of the ailments of his second elderly aunt. Sara had been looking forward to some ice cream, perhaps capturing once more the intensity of flavour she'd experienced at their first meeting.

They bypass the beach and walk silently through the backstreets, probably because he's taking the shortcut home. To bring forward the end of a spectacularly unsuccessful evening.

Fury takes hold of her. She hasn't put up with an unsatisfactory marriage, raised three children, worked her entire life, survived a torrid menopause and the loss of her beloved parents only to allow herself to be defined by a man's tepid response to her appearance, even if said man was her first and most enduring love.

She decides that she will leave Henry and sleep in a hotel room tonight, and every other night of her stay. She will enjoy her expensive, solitary holiday to the best of her ability with her dignity intact, eating dessert every single night. Then go home to the UK and rebuild her shattered life somehow. She's a mature woman. She can do this. She can do anything.

"There's something I want to show you," he says.

She's about to reply when they stop outside a shop she's admired countless times on social media, and through the window she sees a colourful array of flavours. Her resolve to leave him melts away like an abandoned ice cream on hot cement.

These days there's much more than vanilla and passionfruit and chocolate on offer. A blackboard lists paperbark and native honey, peppermint gum and peach, chocolate sapote and orange marmalade, Davidson plum and vanilla bean. It's Henry's business now, and he's an artisan ice cream maker with an international following.

The interior is smart and contemporary, lined with salvaged corrugated iron, painted in soft greens. People sit at bespoke Australian hardwood tables to eat, dripping their ice creams onto a polished concrete floor. Two young women she recognises from photos as Henry's twenty-something daughters serve the queue of customers, their crisp white T-shirts barely concealing their muscular surfers' bodies.

He pulls her towards the door.

"Let's go in," he says.

"But—" She steps away from the bright light of the window, and into the shadows.

"You don't want to?" He takes her face in his hands and looks into her eyes. "I'm so sorry I was late. I was a mess by the time I made it to Arrivals, thinking about how I'd kept you waiting. There was a power failure in the shop, and I panicked, but still, it was careless of me. And to leave my phone at home, because I was excited and nervous, and to be unable to contact you... it was terrible. I understand why you've been unhappy. If only I could make it up to you somehow. This is all I can think of." He gestures towards the shop, then hesitates. "You seemed so distant at the airport, and not yourself, and then you were silent in the car. Perhaps you find me too old now. Too dull. In the winter of my days..."

"No Henry. I thought *I* was the problem."

"You? You could *never* be a problem for me." He takes her into his arms, and she snuggles into his chest. He whispers in her ear, "Still the most beautiful woman in Manly."

They kiss, right there on the street, and it's even better than the first time, like a swirl of the most exquisite flavours imaginable. Sara wants to stay in the safe circle of his arms forever. But it's getting cool outside.

"Do you remember what brought us together all those years ago?" Her body tingles with anticipation.

"Ice cream." The words fall from his lips like another kiss.

He opens the door to the shop, and leads her in.

II
DREAMING OF ICED CREAMS

CAROLINE DENESS

Cambridgeshire 1816

Ellen was glad of the breeze as she tooled the gig up the lane. The oppressive heat undoubtedly presaged a storm. She tried to think cool thoughts — water, snow, ice. Then, most delicious of all, Gunter's iced creams from London.

Not that Ellen had ever tried the treats herself. Her father, the vicar of a parish in the flat fen country, could never afford a London Season for her. Not with five younger children to support and an ailing wife.

Glancing over the hedge at the farmhands scything the wheat, Ellen's breath caught.

A tall, golden-haired man tipped a jug of water over his face. The water splashed down to the open neck of his white shirt, which clung to his muscled torso.

"Oh, my sweet Lord." The words tumbled uncensored from her lips.

The unknown god turned towards her, and as her eyes locked with his, Ellen felt the heat rise to her cheeks, tearing her gaze away only when her horse pulled at the reins in her distracted fingers. She could have sworn fire burned from his eyes to her body. She needed a whole tub of iced confections to cool her response.

Hoping the housekeeper at the Grange had some lemonade, Ellen continued down the lane. She willed her heart rate to slow, as she fought the urge to look back. And called to mind all her father's sermons on self-restraint and her mother's pride in her 'Miss Practical' daughter, to give herself the strength.

Mrs Fielding didn't disappoint when Ellen entered the spacious kitchen.

"Miss Ellen, come in. I bet you'll be glad of a lemonade. I had Mr Fielding dig out some ice from the icehouse for the lads in the fields. It's a hot time they're having getting the crops cut this year."

"Thank you, Mrs F, I'd love a glass. I'm sorry to impose at such a busy time."

"No matter, Miss Ellen, you're always welcome, I'm sure."

"Ah, lovely." The refreshing tang of lemon soothed the last of the heat from Ellen's encounter. "Mama sent me over to beg some of your lotion for her heat rash. She's itching fit to scream. She had to chase the chickens the twins let out the other day." Ellen took a seat at the table and smiled after the grey-haired woman as she bustled into her pantry in search of the remedy.

Fraser Dunblane stared after the raven-haired lass, the memory of her ice-blue gaze still pinning him to the spot. Slowly, the sounds of the other men scything recalled him to the urgency of the harvest. All the locals predicted a storm was inevitable from the sultry heat.

He didn't want the first harvest on his inherited estate ruined, any more than his tenant farmers did.

No doubt his housekeeper would know the lass. Mrs Fielding knew all. He set to work again with a will, but his thoughts soon drifted back to his vision.

"Blistering hell."

A searing pain gripped his left leg as he pulled the scythe back for another stroke. Fraser dropped the blade when he saw the blood welling from a cut above his knee. Bending, he found a long tear in his breeches, and he clamped his hands over the wound. Several minutes later, he acknowledged he would need a good bandage to staunch the bleeding properly, and he headed back to the Grange.

"Sorry, lad, you were right about amateurs and blades. I'll be back as soon as I'm patched up," he called to Tom, his steward, on the way.

Fraser banged into the kitchen from the garden and stopped dead.

"Och, 'tis you," he said, mouth ajar.

ঙ৪৪৩

Ellen looked up as the back door to the kitchen burst open, and in walked her god. *Her god?* Good gracious, what would Papa say?

She watched as a wicked grin appeared above his stubbled chin. His 'och' vibrated in her ears, and his green eyes sparked.

"I knew Mrs Fielding wouldn't let me down about knowing you. Well, lass, welcome to my humble abode."

Ellen sucked in a breath. Finally, she met the new owner of Elm Grange. The light from the door silhouetted his wide shoulders and trim waist.

"You're Major Dunblane?"

"In the flesh."

The devil raised an eyebrow in challenge. Yes, surely he was no god after all, but a temptation sent to test her.

"There y'are, Miss Ellen, I was sure I had some of the lotion hid away. Oh, Major, you're back early. Has something happened?" Mrs Fielding put the salve on the table beside Ellen. "I see you've met Miss Stroud, our vicar's daughter."

"Thanks, Mrs Fielding. I'd say we've seen each other, rather than met." He bowed, elegantly, regardless of his lack of jacket or cravat. "Enchanted, Miss Stroud."

Ellen noticed the Scots burr, just before the blood on his stocking.

"What happened?" Ellen asked, pointing to the blood.

"It seems I'm not as adept at scything as I thought. There are traps for the unwary beginner."

"Oh dear, Major, I'll get some bandages and salve," Mrs Fielding clucked. "Sit you down and put that leg up on a chair."

"Sorry, Mrs F, I didn't mean to bloody your clean floor. I fear I opened an old wound."

As the housekeeper bustled about, the major did as he was told. He sat and removed his heavy boot, and put his stockinged foot up, before applying pressure to the wound.

Ellen rose to take the bowl of warm water and cloth from Mrs Fielding.

"Now, Major, you had better pull your breeches away from the wound, so I can clean it."

"But, Miss Stroud, you shouldne be tending my wound." He looked startled.

"Major, I have five younger siblings. I've tended many wounds."

Colour mottled his face, as he threw a hand up in surrender.

"Very well, lass, if you insist."

Ellen looked at the long clean cut through a ragged scar.

"How did you acquire your scar, Major?"

"A musket ball at Waterloo." His gruff tone made her look up.

"Sorry if it's painful. I think we may need a few stitches here."

"Hell."

അ‍‍ു‍

The pain of the cleaning, as gentle and efficient as Miss Stroud's ministrations were, took Fraser back to the weeks of recovery, after his wound had become infected. To the pain of losing so many of his comrades that day. Hell, indeed.

He almost missed his nurse's question.

"Which regiment did you serve with, Major?"

"The Scots Greys, lass."

Mrs Fielding appeared beside him. Fraser didn't want to discuss his military service, so he smiled up at his housekeeper.

"Do your worst."

"I must be going now, Major." The lass stood and collected the lotion from the table. "Thank you, Mrs F, mother will be relieved to get this."

And then she left.

Fraser felt the loss immediately. *How could that be?*

The heat of the day, and the pain in his leg, had suddenly become oppressive.

CʒꙄ

Ellen's mind refused to leave the subject of Major Dunblane. His intense gaze, his strong body radiated a reassuring aura. His rumbling r's seemed to set up a resonance in her own body. But it was his wicked grin that made her even hotter. Oh, for some of those legendary iced creams.

The lotion soothed her mother's skin.

The sultry heat continued for another two days.

Major Dunblane did not appear at Sunday service. No doubt he was still busy harvesting, she told herself to mask her disappointment.

That night the storm broke. Thunder cracked Ellen awake at midnight. By dawn she was in the kitchen, planning to check the damage before her siblings got themselves into any disasters.

"Mama."

Ellen was brought up short by the sight of her mother's head over a steaming bowl of water. Musical wheezes announced a bad bout of asthma.

"Ellen... dearest..." her mother puffed. "It came on in the storm. I can't find my Jimson weed to smoke." She sucked in a breath. "D'you think Mrs Fielding would have some?"

"I'm sure she will, Mama. I'll go at once."

Mama's shoulders sagged in relief.

Quickly, Ellen hitched the pony to the gig and set off. The going was muddy, but blessedly cool after the storm. She was almost at the Grange when the wheels stuck fast in the mire.

"Bother and blast!"

With no alternative, Ellen climbed down gingerly, trying to find firm footing at the side of the lane. She held up her skirts to avoid the puddles, and rushed along the hedge, eyes on the ground.

"Oomph!" She hit a solid wall. Warm arms closed around her back, and she looked up to find the major with that grin of his in place.

"Eh, lass, you're a fine sight after the storm."

"Major," Ellen whispered, flummoxed by her reaction — she was never flustered. "Major, I'm here for my mother. She is having a bad attack of asthma, and hoping Mrs Fielding has some Jimson weed." She motioned her head back up the lane. "The gig is bogged."

The major stepped back and took his hands off her shoulders.

"Come on then, Ellen lass, no time to lose." He took her hand in his great paw and pulled.

CRT80

Fraser was delighted to have bumped, literally, into Miss Stroud. He had been dreaming of her at night. A very pleasant reprieve from nightmares of screaming horses and cannon fire, even if he had woken in a state of longing.

While Mrs Fielding searched her larder, Fraser called for his big horse, Storm, to be saddled, and for someone to rescue the pony in the lane.

"There y'are, Miss Ellen." Mrs Fielding handed over the package. "I hope your dear mother is better soon."

Fraser grasped Ellen's hand. "C'mon, lass, we'll ride over the fields. 'T'will be much quicker." He led her out the door as she thanked the housekeeper.

Lifting her onto the saddle, Fraser leapt up behind, settled her comfortably across his legs, and urged Storm to an easy canter.

"Dinna worry, Ellen lass, I have you." Fraser sighed in satisfaction to have her to himself. Holding her in his arms felt natural. He would have chuckled, except she was so worried about her Mama. He had never dreamed he could feel so content.

CRT80

Sitting, cradled by the major's arms, Ellen felt as though she was back in the summer's heat. Her heart thumped a tattoo to the horse's hooves. Surely iced creams would melt in her vicinity?

"Oh no, Major, what about my pony in the lane?" She'd completely forgotten the poor beast. What had happened to her orderly mind? It flew into tangles in his proximity. She hardly dared look him in the face.

"I sent a groom to rescue him, lass." The glow in his eyes, as he looked down at her, stole her breath.

"Thank you," she managed. "I'm usually the one organising rescues. You must think me a ninny."

"No, lass, never that. You're worried about your Mama. Canna quibble with that."

Thank goodness they were almost at the vicarage. Ellen was ready to burst into flames of embarrassment and she knew not what. Pulling his horse up at the gate, the major jumped down, before helping Ellen off the huge animal.

"Is this one of your Scots Greys?" The irrelevant thought popped right out. Ellen barely saw the nod as she rushed to the kitchen.

Grabbing up the old pipe, Ellen put it and the package of dried leaves beside her mother. Then she reached for a taper to light at the stove.

Her mother's blue lips told their own tale, as she gasped her thanks.

Loading the pipe, Ellen set it at her mother's mouth and put the flame to the leaves. Her mother struggled to suck in the smoke. Gradually the wheezes eased, and her lips lost their blue tinge.

Ellen's shoulders lowered, the tension easing in her body. "Thank the Lord," she breathed, just as the back door opened, and the now-familiar silhouette appeared.

"Major, thank you. Mama is already improving. Mama, this is Major Dunblane from the Grange. He brought me back because the gig was bogged."

A sweet smile formed on her mother's face. "Thank you, Major, you saved me. You and Ellen."

"'T'was my pleasure, Mrs Stroud. I'm very happy to meet you. I can see where your daughter gets her lovely smile."

The rascal lifted her mother's limp hand and raised it to his lips. Ellen's eyes caught on those mobile lips.

Heavens, where were her wits wandering?

"Where is Papa? Is no-one with you? The house seems very quiet."

"Mrs Jacob's husband just died, and her son came to get your father. I said you'd be back soon, so he took John with him, and left Meg with the other boys."

Just then a thundering sounded in the hall, and a tornado of seven-year-old twins and their nine-year-old brother burst into the kitchen.

"I'm sorry, Mama," Meg followed her brothers in. "They saw the big horse from the window and had to investigate."

The boys stopped in front of the major and stared up at him. He grinned down and ruffled the twins' hair.

"What's all that noise, ye wee scamps? Yer poor mother needs some quiet."

The boys shuffled their feet, but kept staring.

"Sorry, Mama."

Stepping in, Ellen called the boys to order. "Meg, boys, this is Major Dunblane from the Grange. Major, my sister Margaret and my brothers. Make your bows, boys." Meg curtsied prettily.

"If ye wish to say hello to Storm, ye may go meet him in the stable. But no running, lads. He's friendly if you approach him quietly."

The boys nodded solemnly at the major, clearly mesmerised. Mumbling their assurances, they headed out the door.

"Perhaps you should go with them, Major. I'm not sure they know the meaning of 'quietly'."

"Aye, lass, if you'll come with me for protection?" He sent her a pleading look.

"I am sure you could manage three small boys all by yourself, Major, but we shouldn't detain you. I'll see you out," Ellen said, shaking her head at his silliness.

As the major said his goodbyes to her family, Ellen went ahead to rescue the horse.

Before she reached the stable, however, Fraser caught up with her. Taking her hand, he slowed her pace.

"You have a delightful family, lass. Reminds me of home, in Scotland. I never thought to feel at ease amongst Sassenachs, even though me mam was born here." She saw his face soften. "Yer ma's illness must be a worry, lass. It seems you're the one to look after her."

"But, naturally, Major. I'm the eldest, so it falls to me."

"What about your father?"

"He's always being called out by parishioners, and he hates to see Mama in difficulty." Ellen shrugged. What could she do?

"Have you never wished for someone to help you?" His murmur sent tingles through her entire body. Time to think of iced creams again.

As Fraser rode back to his new home, all he could think about was helping his wee lass. He was shocked at how quickly he had become so protective. And even more so, after his faith in humanity had been so shaken by Waterloo. Nevertheless, he wanted to relieve Ellen of her cares.

To make her happy.

To make her his.

He wasn't sure exactly how Ellen felt about him, but he was hopeful she felt some attraction. He could work with that.

He was surprised when an invitation to dinner at the vicarage arrived next morning. Perhaps he had an ally in Mrs Stroud? He was certainly keen to see how the vicar measured up.

Ellen went about her chores at the vicarage the next day, with uncharacteristic inattention: burning her hand as she poured tea for her mama, who thankfully, was breathing normally again; tripping over shoes discarded by one of her brothers.

Where were her wits? Wandering way too often to the major.

He was a wicked temptation, she told herself. Much better to think of iced creams — something she *might* try one day.

As she set the table for dinner, Mama entered. "Set an extra place for the major, will you, Ellen?"

"What?" The cutlery clattered to the table.

Before she could take a breath, there was a knock at the front door. Oh, my heavens, was it him?

"Go answer the door, Ellen, I'll finish this."

"Major," she breathed, as his body filled the door frame.

"Good evening, lass," he purred, as he took her hand and raised it to his lips. She shivered, then realised the thundering noise was not her heart (or not just), but her hellion brothers.

"Major, can we go and see Storm?" they choroused.

"Aye, lads, off ye go."

Mama filled the vacuum left by the departing boys.

"Good evening, Major. Ellen, why don't you take the major for a turn in the garden until dinner?"

"I would enjoy that, Mrs Stroud. And I'm happy to see you well." The major bowed.

Ellen's heart did thunder, as she led the major out. He tucked her hand in his elbow, and heat spread from there.

"Eh, lass, you look heated. How can I cool you off?" His grin only elevated her temperature.

"Major, you must stop this. I'm spending my life thinking of Gunter's iced creams, to cool off, ever since I met you. And I've never even eaten one."

"Well, lass, we could remedy that. But *I've* been dreaming of your sweet lips. Only you can help me with that." He drew her behind a large rhododendron bush and looked down into her eyes. Hope shone from his green ones.

Could she?

Should she?

"Yes." And he covered her burning lips with his.

Cool and sweet.

Bliss.

So much better than dreams of iced creams. She didn't even notice the heat.

12

G IS FOR GELATO

VALERIE G MILLER

W hen she saw the *Frame your Love* competition with a prize of a ten-day trip for two to Italy, Aubrey Jones couldn't believe her eyes. Ever since she was a little girl, listening to her mum's stories about Italy, she had always wanted to go there. Even more so after her mum had passed away.

This was her chance to satisfy her obsession with everything Italian: food, history, fashion, and maybe even meeting a handsome Italian man who'd whisk her away for a romantic weekend at Positano. Just like Frances in *Under the Tuscan Sun*.

She couldn't wait to tell her bestie and neighbour, Lilian, all about it. Texting quickly, she wrote: "*Come 2 pool after work. I'm bringing Prosecco.*"

⚬⚬⚬

"Oh my gawd! Aubrey! This is great news. You must be so excited."

Aubrey poured more bubbly and said "I know. I can't believe

it. I keep pinching myself."

"Well, my fingers are crossed for you. When you want to achieve something, you just go for it." Lilian clinked glasses with Aubrey. "I really hope you win."

"Yeah, me too!" Aubrey laughed, saying, "But there are a few stipulations."

"Like what?"

"Well, there is a tight timeline to get everything done, plus I have to find the perfect guy to pretend to be my fiancé." Aubrey giggled and sipped her Prosecco.

"Who do you have in mind? Darren at work?"

"Ewww. No. I need someone handsome, preferably with dark hair — Italian looking. Darren probably thinks ravioli is something that comes in a can."

"Ladies, you know you're not supposed to have glass in the pool area."

Aubrey and Lilian turned to find their neighbour Henry jokingly wagging his finger at them.

"Oh, don't be a stick-in-the-mud, Henry," Aubrey said, smiling at him. "Come and join us. The wine is chilled."

"Love to, but I can't. I have an assignment due for uni, and I have to polish some copy for a client. Maybe next time."

"Well, don't work too hard," Aubrey said, her eyes following him as he walked into the apartment block. She sighed and turned back to Lilian, who was giving her a pointed look, complete with raised eyebrows.

"What?"

"Oh, my God, you like him."

"Maybe." Aubrey smiled as she focused on her glass of bubbly.

Lilian's eyes widened. "It's him. Henry. He's your guy."

Aubrey nodded.

"He's definitely handsome in a broody kind of way, but how are you going to get him to agree? Isn't he a bit of a loner?"

"He's just shy. We got talking at the residents" Christmas party. He's from the country — Maleny. His family runs a dairy farm. He's super busy, doing a degree and working. He works from home. I think he's a copywriter. And he's intelligent and interesting. He'd make a great travelling partner. Plus, he's perfect for the photo shoot."

"What photo shoot?"

Aubrey leaned in close to Lilian. "I have to submit photos of us together."

"For the competition?" Lilian's eyes widened.

"Yep. I've got it all planned, and I've done a storyboard. My theme's Gelato. Ice cream, a scooter, summer... all pastels."

"Of course you have." Lilian laughed.

"I've got a studio booked, and today I hired a pale pink Vespa. The gelato shop next door is going to comp the ice cream and cones."

"Now, what's taking you so long?" Lilian joked. "But wait, what happens if he says no?"

Aubrey leaned back on the deckchair and glanced over at the pool.

"I've got a plan."

⊂⑅⊃

Aubrey stood outside Henry's apartment. She pushed the rogue curl out of her face and smoothed her favourite dress. The 1950s style emphasised her waist and gave her an alluring feminine look. She just wished her wild mane would behave itself, but her blonde curls had a mind of their own.

She stood close to the door. Ed Sheeran's smooth voice harmonised inside. Promising. He was home, and he liked romantic music.

She knocked on the door and waited.

Nothing. She sighed.

Aubrey knocked again. Still nothing.

Was he ignoring her? Was he peeking through the peephole right now?

Aubrey turned to go when the door flew open. Henry stood in the doorway, his wavy hair dripping, and his toned body wrapped in a towel. Aubrey tried to remain calm as the blood pounded in her ears. She had not expected this.

"Oh, hi. It's you." Henry tightened his grip on the towel.

Aubrey's words came out in a stutter. She'd never been lost for words before, but Henry looked so sexy that her tongue tripped over itself. She could feel herself blushing, knowing her chest was beet red. "I'm sorry... I can come back later. If that's okay. If you want. I mean... is that okay?"

Henry smiled.

That smile changed the way he looked. He was striking, in a messy, rugged way. She wondered what it would be like to reach up and stroke his stubble.

He was speaking to her.

"Sorry... I..., uh, didn't catch that."

"I said, come in. I'll throw some clothes on."

He opened the door wider, inviting Aubrey inside.

As he went to get dressed, Aubrey looked around the sparsely furnished apartment. Minimalist. A total dude's style — requisite large desk with two computer screens. A massive bookcase, filled with classics and foreign literature, took up one complete wall. She smiled at the photo of his family on the kitchen counter.

"I just made coffee. Would you like some?" Henry returned, dressed in a pair of jeans and a brown t-shirt with 'PANTS' stamped across the front.

"Yes, please." Aubrey settled on one of the two chrome stools at the counter. She pointed at his t-shirt. "That's funny. I can see irony's your thing."

"Yeah, my brothers and I have a funny t-shirt competition at Christmas."

"Did that one win?"

"No. My eldest brother, Ethan, won with a *T. rex* saying: *If you're happy & you know it, clap your, dot, dot, dot. Oh.*"

Aubrey laughed.

He handed her a mug of coffee, pushed a pile of novels to the side and set out the milk and sugar.

Aubrey picked up Hemingway's collection of short stories. "You do like your classics."

"I do." He leaned against a bank of cupboards and sipped his coffee. "So, what can I do for you?"

Aubrey's nerves tangled and made her chest feel tight. This was not like her. She was always forthright. As a personal shopper for a high-end department store, she made snap decisions all the time.

But now, with Henry standing there, looking every kind of delicious, she didn't feel as confident. She was saved by the bell — literally — when his phone began playing the first bars of Pink Floyd's 'Time'.

Henry checked the phone. "Sorry, gotta take this." He stepped over to his home office area.

Aubrey looked around the apartment, trying not to eavesdrop, but suddenly her ears pricked up.

"No, Maddie. I can't right now." Henry glanced over to Aubrey, and then averted his eyes.

Aubrey's heart plummeted. Of course, Henry had a girlfriend. Why wouldn't he? He was gorgeous. Now she felt like a right nitwit.

"Can we talk about this later?" He ran his hand through his hair, clearly uncomfortable.

Maddie was not taking no for an answer. Aubrey looked at the door. She needed to get out of here — not now, but right now.

With exaggerated hand signals, Aubrey indicated to Henry that she was leaving. Avoiding eye contact, she opened the door and closed it softly behind her.

෨෫෨

Back in her apartment, she paced back and forth, feeling horribly embarrassed. Her silly, bruised pride slunk off to the corner. How could she have been so presumptuous?

She looked in the hall mirror. Her cheeks were flushed, and she was hyperventilating.

What did she think would happen? That he'd say yes? Sweep her off her feet? Propose? Fly her to Tuscany for the wedding?

Aubrey grabbed her phone and flung herself on the sofa. What a mess.

Maddie! Yeah, right.

She could picture her. Tall, leggy, with long shiny brunette hair.

Aubrey punched the screen, and when she heard Lilian's voice, she unleashed.

"Oh, my God, Lilian. I'm so embarrassed. I've just come

from Henry's apartment. I was going to ask him if he'd be interested in doing the photo shoot. Then I got scared, which is not like me. And then he took a call. I just tried to be invisible. I checked out his apartment. Which is really neat, by the way. Then I heard him say, 'Maddie'."

Aubrey took a deep breath and continued.

"I mean, I'm an idiot. Why *wouldn't* he have a girlfriend? Look at him. I stood there, smiling at him, like I'm a few sandwiches short of a picnic. Finally, I found some sense of dignity to get my act together, and I left. Oh Lilian, what am I going to do? I really had my heart set on Henry. I need someone who looks good. Now I'll have to ask Dorky Darren. God, I'm such a goof."

Before Lilian had a chance to say one word, Aubrey heard a knock on her door.

"Lilian!" she whispered. "There's someone at my front door."

"Why are you whispering? Go and see who it is," Lilian replied. "Call me back."

Aubrey flung the door open and was surprised to see Henry standing there.

"I'm sorry about that," Henry apologised. "The call took longer than I expected."

Aubrey studied his face. He had a little crease above his nose she wanted to smooth out. Instead, she crossed her arms and leaned against the doorjamb.

"You didn't get a chance to say why you dropped by," he continued.

Aubrey considered the situation. She still needed a pretend fiancé for the photo shoot. And he was good-looking with his dark features. Rugged and sexy. The photos would be gorgeous. To hell with Maddie! She plunged ahead.

"I don't know if your girlfriend would approve, but I wanted to ask if you would help me out and be in a photo shoot with me." She rubbed her sweaty palms down her dress.

He studied her quietly with his pale blue eyes.

"It's okay if you don't." Aubrey felt her face burn... again. "I mean, I wouldn't if I had a boyfriend like—" She stopped. *Shut up Aubrey.*

Henry's laugh surprised her. "You mean the call. Maddie? No. She's not my girlfriend. Not anymore."

"Oh. I'm sorry." Now Aubrey felt silly.

"Trust me. Nothing to be sorry about. It turned out I'm not her type." He leaned in close. "You know. Bookish."

Aubrey smiled. At least he had a sense of humour.

He broke into an open, friendly smile. "I'd love to be in the photo shoot. It sounds like fun."

ᚗ

For the next week, Henry and Aubrey spent time together planning and preparing. He had some great creative ideas. A couple of times, when their hands or legs touched, Aubrey felt the electricity. Henry remained friendly, but cool. She kept reminding herself that this was professional... nothing more was going on.

Too bad her emotions weren't getting the message.

She worked hard to remain neutral and businesslike, but it was difficult. However, she got to know a little more about Henry. She discovered he was intelligent and warm, with a dry sense of humour. He made her laugh.

A couple of days before the photo shoot, Aubrey came home to find a note from Henry taped on her front door asking her to come over.

She knocked, and the smell of homemade pizza and garlic wafted from the apartment when he opened the door.

"What's all this?"

Henry grabbed her hand, and her heart tingled. He looked so pleased with himself.

La Dolce Vita's opening scene sat frozen on the TV, ready to watch. Two wine glasses and a bottle of Chianti sat on the coffee table.

"Sit. Relax."

"Something smells great." Aubrey poured herself a glass of wine and one for Henry.

"I made pizza. With mozzarella, olives and prosciutto." He rubbed his hands together. "You can't get more Italian than that." He winked.

"No, you can't." Aubrey laughed as she sipped her wine. "This wine is delicious. Great choice."

While they ate, Henry told Aubrey he was in the middle of two brothers — the youngest was a world-champion equestrian, and his older brother was a well-known heart surgeon.

"I'm the black sheep." Henry laughed, but Aubrey saw something else in his eyes.

"I'm not in their league, but I'm working hard at uni and getting some pretty good results. I want to become an architect. Maybe be the next Harry Seidler."

"That's cool. I'm a personal shopper right now, but eventually I want to get into marketing. This contest might help me."

As they watched the movie, Aubrey moved into a more comfortable position, tucking her legs up and yawning. "Sorry, I'm a little tired. Too much wine."

Henry patted his shoulder, and Aubrey rested her head against him. They both watched as Sylvia, the heroine, waded into the Trevi Fountain.

Aubrey's heart flipped when their fingers fumbled together, reaching into the popcorn. A giggle seeped out and she tucked her hair behind her ear. The tension sizzled — and not just on the TV — when Henry grabbed a piece of popcorn caught in her curls. He smelled so good. Her whole body fizzed. She really, really liked being around him.

ⒼⓈ⅋ⓈⒹ

Aubrey stood in front of the studio, clutching a garment bag full of clothes. Her makeup and hair had been done to give it a 1950s, Audrey Hepburn crossed with Gina Lollobrigida look.

She glanced at her watch. Henry was late — really late. She bit her bottom lip and her heart pounded. *What if he doesn't show? What if he changed his mind? What if something happened?* Irrational thoughts jack-hammered in her mind.

Just as panic set in, an Uber pulled up in front of her, and Henry jumped out. Warm relief flooded through her.

"I'm sorry I'm late." He held up his own suit bag. "I told mum about the shoot and she got really excited. She pulled out my granddad's old clothes, had them cleaned and delivered them! They're perfect."

Aubrey's heart threatened to burst. She willed the tears back; she'd spent too much money on her makeup.

"Thank you," she whispered instead.

Cameron, their photographer, took a few test photos and was proving to be worth every cent of his fee. He had them look and move in different ways to get them relaxed. Aubrey was surprised at how nervous she felt, and how comfortable Henry seemed. Every time Henry touched her — a brush of his arm, a press of his leg, or when he placed his arm around her for one of the shots — her insides did flips as mini fireworks exploded around her heart.

Aubrey became utterly besotted when she sat in front of him

on the Vespa, eating a strawberry gelato while his muscular arms wrapped around her waist. She was worried the heat she was feeling would make the ice cream melt all over her new dress. She caught herself nuzzling against him, then stopped when she realised what she was doing, but Henry pulled her back.

Was he feeling the electricity, too? Bubbles of excitement made her feel giddy, and she giggled.

"That's a wrap," Cameron called out, still clicking off shots. "It's easy to tell you two are in love," he added enthusiastically.

Aubrey felt embarrassed at the comment and was glad she was facing away from Henry. She should've been ecstatic that even their photographer thought they were a couple, and in love. This is exactly what she'd planned for.

Then it hit her.

Hard.

She realised she didn't want to pretend anymore. She really wanted her and Henry to be a couple.

Aubrey was falling, headfirst, in love with Henry.

When Cameron finished taking the photos, he pulled up the images on his laptop.

"These are fantastic!" Aubrey clapped her hands with glee.

Henry stood quietly as he studied the photos.

"Don't you like them?"

"I do." He looked at Aubrey. His eyes smouldered with passion. Aubrey wanted to reach up and touch his face.

Cameron interrupted Aubrey's reverie. "Why don't we take some fun photos."

With fresh ice cream cones, they stood in front of the Vespa and the tension between them shifted. Aubrey was frozen to the spot. She looked towards the camera like a deer in the headlights. Henry tapped her on the shoulder, and she turned to him. There was a broad, mischievous grin plastered on his face. He offered her a taste of his chocolate gelato as the camera clicked away. As she went to take a bite, he rubbed it on her cheek.

She stood there. Shocked. Then burst out laughing before smearing her pistachio ice cream down Henry's stubble.

"You didn't." Henry feigned an I'm-going-to-get-you look, and ran his cone down her nose. He leaned in and kissed her.

Aubrey wrapped her arms around Henry's neck and, with a face covered in chocolate ice cream, she returned his kiss slowly, relishing every sweet second.

She giggled when she heard Cameron's excitement at capturing a natural and fun moment.

Henry pulled away and looked deep into Aubrey's eyes. Nuzzling into her hair, he whispered, "This is for an authentic Italian experience." Aubrey took a deep breath when she felt Henry's hand press hard against her hip before outlining the shape of her bum.

She squealed when he pinched her.

"Perfect! That's a wrap!" Cameron called.

Henry winked at her. "I think we've satisfied the conditions of the competition."

Aubrey smiled as Henry wiped ice cream off her face and kissed her again.

Did she need a trip to Italy when she already had first prize?

13
THE BRIDGE
KAAREN SUTCLIFFE

The minute Akiko saw the bridge over the inlet, her chest tightened. Miki skipped ahead, oblivious, and she persuaded her feet to keep trudging through the small car park and to take the steps down onto the wooden slats. How had this been a good idea? Satoru had loved coming here. Stopping to lean on the bridge railing, she forced air into her chest. You'd think that after three years she'd be able to cope with the memories. Turquoise water flowed under the bridge, destined for Lake Mummuga. Mid-tide; good for swimming.

"Fish!" shrieked Miki, pounding back over the narrow bridge at full tilt. The girl hooked her arms over the top of the railing and leaned back. "And a manta!"

Akiko peered at the mottled brown and beige stingray drifting over the sandy floor. "There goes another one." She pointed at a smaller stingray trailing after the first one.

"Aww, cute. Must be a baby," said Miki with a wise nod.

A shoal of pale silver fish flitted under the bridge. Akiko swallowed. Satoru would have grunted with pleasure and raced over the bridge to the beach to cast his line into the surf, ever hopeful of catching their dinner. Taking a deep breath, she pushed her long black hair back over her shoulders and straightened up. Satoru wasn't here, and Miki deserved to enjoy their short holiday.

She craned her head up at the clear blue sky. It was a gorgeous March day, and they were here to have fun.

"Let's put our towels down, then you can wade." Akiko took Miki's hand.

At the end of the wooden bridge, she took the immediate right-hand path onto the flat sandy oval between the channel of the inlet and the open Dalmeny Beach. The morning sea breeze hadn't yet risen, and she chose a spot not too far from the edge of the channel, from where she'd be able to keep an eye on Miki. On a weekday there weren't many people about. A group of retirees clad in walking gear clumped across the bridge and kept going to the beach. Across the channel, and on the far side of the bike path, the camping ground was mainly vivid green grass with only a handful of tents and caravans.

She spread out their towels, and placed the bucket and spade at one end. Miki kicked off her sandals and started to run. Akiko sat down and watched Miki racing towards a flock of seagulls sitting on the warm sand by the water. A silhouette of a tall man came striding around the corner from the beach, the eastern light shimmering across the sea behind him. The man walked towards her, following the rim of the channel.

Her daughter, black hair flying behind, flung her arms up and sprinted at the closest seagull. The whole flock of twenty rose with raucous shrieks and hovered at head height. Breath held, Akiko willed them to dart across the water. The rowdy flock spun around and flew straight at the man-silhouette. He ducked with a curse and his arms flailed as he struggled to catch something. *Oh no.*

Akiko leaped to her feet and jogged across the sand.

"I'm so sorry!" she called as she drew nearer. "Miki! Come here."

She stopped a few paces away from the man. Wearing beige cargo shorts and a navy t-shirt, his head was tilted down and he scrubbed at the front of his shorts. Akiko swallowed. The man had ice-cream splattered down the front of his shirt and onto his crotch.

Feeling her presence, the man looked up and stopped wiping at his crotch, a pink stain creeping up his neck. "Oh. Hello."

"I'm deeply sorry. My daughter didn't realise..." Akiko bowed to her waist. Given the location of the spilt ice-cream she could hardly offer to help.

The man smiled and lifted his shoulders in a shrug. "Clothes can be washed. Kids need to have fun."

Akiko smiled back. He was being too kind. Behind him, Miki was slinking back sideways, like a crab. "Miki, come and apologise. You made this man drop his ice-cream."

Miki edged around the man and took her hand.

"Bow," hissed Akiko. Miki bowed, but then giggled. Presuming this was due to the location of the spilled ice-cream, Akiko gave the man a wobbling smile. "She is sorry, really."

The man shook Miki's hand. "Hello, Miki. My name is Kraig. With a K." He stood taller, turned clear blue-grey eyes on her and lifted an eyebrow. With his high cheekbones and handsome, square face he looked teasingly familiar.

"I'm Akiko," she said hurriedly. "Er, can I buy you a replacement ice-cream?"

His eyes twinkled. "Only if you both join me with ice-creams."

"Can I have chocolate?" said Miki before Akiko could respond.

Kraig gave Miki a serious look. "Absolutely. And for you?"

The kindness in his eyes made her heart flutter. She shook her head. "I doubt they have my favourite: green tea ice-cream." Remembering that her purse was sitting on the kitchen bench-top, her pulse raced and her cheeks flamed. "I might have to buy your ice-cream tomorrow." She ignored Miki's forming pout. "I didn't bring any money with me."

Kraig raised both eyebrows. "Okay, deal. I'll get today's ice-creams and you can get them tomorrow. I'll be back shortly." He saluted at Miki and marched away towards the bridge.

"Am I in trouble? He's nice." Miki scuffed a bare foot over the sand. "Can I still wade?"

Tempted to say "Yes to all three", Akiko said, "Yes, wade before he comes back."

She plopped down onto her towel and hugged her knees to her chest. It wasn't even 9 a.m. on their first morning and this had happened. Perhaps this Kraig wouldn't come back; perhaps he was only being polite. Her pulse skipped a few beats. *If* he came back, she'd take it as a sign, a good omen. He was tall, kind, handsome, looked fit and capable... and the way his hair curled at his nape... *Stop!*

Watching Miki ploughing through the water at thigh-depth, she sighed. It was such a shame Satoru couldn't see his daughter, who was growing up so fast. In last night's Zoom call, her parents had pressed persuasively for her to go back to Japan. Did she want to? Miki loved Australia and had made friends at school, but it was hard here with no husband and no other family.

Closing her eyes, she enjoyed the warmth in the early sun on her face and arms. She visualised the healing golden light drawing her stress and loneliness out through her skin and floating it away to the canopy of blue sky.

A shadow fell across her and she jumped.

"Here you are." Kraig handed her a cone with pale green ice-cream, juggling a chocolate one and a creamy-yellow one in his other hand.

Akiko stared at the swirl of pale green: it looked like green tea ice-cream, but that was unlikely. Not from the tiny Dalmeny shopping complex. She took a tentative lick. Not too sweet, a delicate, faintly nutty flavour.

"Pistachio," said Kraig. "Is it okay? I guessed that you'd prefer something less sweet." Miki ran up to claim her chocolate cone with an enthusiastic grin and polite thank you.

Akiko took another lick. Should she be offended this Kraig thought she didn't like sweet things? Did she come across as stern? Maybe she should lighten up a bit. "Thanks." She smiled up at him. "In Japan we'd say 'oishii' or delicious."

Kraig unfolded a towel from over his arm, laid it out next to hers and sat down. He also seemed to be wearing a different pair of shorts. He licked his ice-cream and a hint of banana wafted across.

"Do you live here?" The question popped out before she could think about it.

"Yup. Just up over the crest, opposite the headland."

"Can you see the sea from your house?" She thought of the view of the Bay of Ise from her grandmother's house.

"Sure can. I never tire of the view." Kraig rolled his tongue over the top of his ice-cream. "You're from Japan? Visiting, or do you live here?"

"We moved here seven years ago. For now, I live in Canberra." Was she imagining that he looked surprised and then pleased?

"How old is Miki?" Kraig waved his cone at Miki, who had demolished hers and was working on a sandcastle.

"Six." At his thoughtful expression, she added, "Yes, she should be in school today." He turned intense, encouraging eyes on her, and more words tumbled out. "We needed a break, and I felt this was more important." The niggling idea that he looked familiar refused to dissipate, but she was sure she hadn't met him before. She'd have remembered!

Kraig concentrated on finishing his ice-cream, but she sensed him building up to another question. Finally, he put his arms around his knees and looked at her. "Can I ask... Miki's father?"

Her heart pounded. He wanted to know! She peered at him from beneath her dark eyelashes. "Satoru was a research scientist at the university. The ANU sponsored us to come here to live, seven years ago." She chewed her lower lip. "He died in a late-night car accident. Three years ago, today."

"I'm sorry. That's tough." Kraig reached over and briefly patted her shoulder.

His hand felt warm, strong, capable. The urge to lean against him was so powerful she had to look away.

Hugging his knees again, he said softly, "My wife and I split up four years ago. She was pregnant, and we lost the baby." He shrugged. "Somehow, things went downhill from there."

Akiko glanced sideways. He looked stoic, self-contained, but she could see his hurt. Was he deliberately telling her he was available? "I'm sorry, for you." She tried a smile. "We are both... sabishii."

He twisted to look at her. "Sabishii... does that mean sad?"

Her heart raced at the interest on his face. "Sad isn't quite strong enough. It's more like... empty soul."

Kraig frowned, looking even more handsome. His brows lifted. "Melancholy? How about melancholy?"

"Melancholy." She rolled the word around her tongue, careful to pronounce the 'l' sounds. "It means adrift, lost? Yes, we are melancholy."

Kraig smiled, showing neat, white teeth, and his eyes grew lighter. "Well, I reckon melancholy is cured by ice-cream, but only on the beach." He flicked a glance at his watch. "Oh, man. I've got to go." He squeezed her shoulder. "I'm late for work. But you owe me ice-cream tomorrow morning." He jumped up. "Around 8.30 is good. You'll come?"

When she nodded, Kraig smiled, grabbed his towel, waved at Miki and jogged away in a straight line to the bridge.

Akiko watched him jog across the bridge and bound up the steps, then keep jogging through the car park with well-defined, muscled legs and square, strong shoulders. Handsome and likes Miki. Should she come back at 8.30 a.m.?

CREO

Gulls were calling, and primrose light flooded through the window. Akiko stretched out in the bed, an ache lingering in her chest and between her legs. Maybe she shouldn't go to the inlet with ice-creams. Her dreams of being held and kissed by Kraig were disconcerting enough. What would her family think? But they were far away, and Miki liked him. She'd prattled on about the seagull incident and the kind man over dinner — and her choice of strawberry for today's ice-cream.

Miki bounced into the bedroom in her swimmers and climbed onto the bed. "Come on, Mama! Beach!"

Fine. She was going. The bridge of ice-cream beckoned... may it not melt like an illusion. Akiko gulped down a cup of tea, and donned her running shorts and a cherry blossom pink tank top. A walk after the ice-cream would do her good.

Armed with cones of banana and strawberry ice-cream, she padded across the bridge, her sandals slapping the wooden slats. Miki skipped across, pointing to either side at fish or stingrays. Aquamarine water eased below, reflecting another azure March sky. The sandy oval between the bridge and the channel was deserted, and Akiko went that way again.

She passed the strawberry cone to Miki and ambled along the edge of the channel. A cold drop plopped onto her hand. Hopefully, Kraig would appear before she had to eat the banana cone herself. Miki vanished around the curve, the open sea coruscated silvery-blue and the pale golden sand remained deserted. Akiko swallowed her disappointment. Never mind, she could still walk a lap of the beach.

A tall silhouette strode around the bend and marched towards her, the shorter silhouette of Miki skipping around him. Her pulse raced. They looked so comfortable, so good *together*. She chewed her lip: best not get ahead of herself here.

"Morning! Thanks," Kraig relieved her of the dripping banana ice-cream. He took some hasty bites of the gooey parts and then mumbled, "I'm glad you came."

A shiver chased down her spine at the way his eyes roamed over her hair and face. He looked over her attire, and she swallowed when his eyes widened and one eyebrow lifted.

"Looks like you're dressed for action. Let's walk?" His voice sounded deep and husky.

With a nod, she fell in beside him when he turned and headed back to the open beach. Miki raced ahead, halting randomly to peer at shells along the shore.

"I hope you didn't get in trouble for being late yesterday?"

Kraig gave her a serious look. "The captain was furious! Gave me a right bollocking."

Anxiety shot through her. "Oh, so sorry. My fault." Wait, did he say 'captain'? "Do you work on a boat?"

Kraig grinned. "Actually, I'm the captain and I own the boat. My crew laughed when I told them what happened."

This handsome, capable man was a boat captain... for an instant the sea and sky tilted and Akiko felt faint.

"Are you alright?" Kraig stopped and peered at her.

Heart pounding erratically, she said, "Yes, it's just... I love boats."

"You do?" Kraig's mouth dropped open. "Oh, wow." He ran a hand through his short, brown hair. "My ex-wife hated boats. Hated me diving, thought it was risky."

"You're a diver?" Her veins pulsed with excitement. "My family is from Ise, in southern Japan." She observed his face closely. "My grandmother is an Ama diver. There are only two thousand left now."

"Seriously?" He looked skyward. "This is incredible! I once read an article about the Ama divers. Is it true they dive free, no equipment, none at all, and can hold their breath for two minutes? And they fetch pearls or abalone?"

He grabbed both of her elbows. "Can you dive like that, with no equipment? You must come out on my boat. She's berthed at Narooma, and we do tours, snorkelling and diving near Montague Island." He waved his hand at the strip of island, visible from the beach.

"There's a colony of seals, several actually, many species of fish and in spring there are whales." His cheeks flushed. "I'm getting carried away. I'm a marine biologist."

Akiko laughed. "We'd love to come on your boat."

Miki skipped a circle around them. "We're going on a boat! Can we see a whale?"

"Not in March." Kraig ruffled Miki's hair. "You see them in May, when they swim north." He looked at Akiko. "If you come in May, we can go look for them." His lips curved in a tentative, lop-sided smile. "September to October they migrate back south, with their whale calves. You could come back then, too."

"I want to see the baby whales!" shrieked Miki, spinning around and around. "Can we, Mama?"

Looking up at Kraig, Akiko said, "I expect so." She tilted her head. "Tell me why you look familiar."

Kraig blinked at the sudden change of topic. Then he gave a mischievous smile. "I'm told I look like Jason Bourne."

Frowning, Akiko ran her mind over her small circle of work colleagues, and Satoru's from the university. "I don't know a Jason Bourne."

Kraig laughed, a rich, carefree sound. "Good, because he's an assassin!"

"What?" She covered her mouth with a hand.

"I'm messing with you. He's a character in the movies based on the books by Robert Ludlum." Kraig laughed again.

"Oh. I've seen the books in the library, where I work." Relief gushed through her. "I haven't seen the movies, though."

"The actor's name is Matt Damon," Kraig said slowly. "Perhaps you've seen him in something else? *Ford vs Ferrari*? *The Promised Land*? *Hereafter* or *The Martian*?"

Akiko gasped. "*The Martian*, a few times. Satoru liked the science in that movie." She took in Kraig's hair, cheekbones, square jaw, blue-grey eyes, the lop-sided smile that she would so like to kiss... her own Matt Damon. With a boat. She could indeed come to Dalmeny often — it was only a three-hour drive south from Canberra. The spirit of Satoru might even approve. Her grandmother certainly would.

Kraig took Miki's hand and reached his free hand out to her. "Let's walk to the rocks."

With a nervous swallow, she slipped her hand into his, liking the way he closed his fingers over hers. Her feet enjoying the warm, firm sand, she opened her ears to the pounding of the surf and the cries of the sea birds. Pistachio ice-cream was not green tea ice-cream, but it tasted good. Kraig was not Satoru, but her heart was skipping and her body quivering.

The jutting rocks were a kilometre away — plenty of time to find out more about Kraig — and savour this new feeling.

14

DREAMS, SCHEMES AND ICE-CREAM

ANNETTE LEIGH

Izzy had never dreamed she'd be mystery-shopping her way around the Aegean. But here she was, on the cruise ship *Contessa* anchored off Santorini, being paid to try, buy and give feedback to the cruise company. So far, she'd given a big tick of approval to the Broadway-worthy shows, all fifteen restaurants, a selection of day tours and the nightclub. The only thing yet to receive a big tick on the evaluation sheet was the ice-cream kiosk. Romance didn't have a tick either, but it wasn't on the list.

Deacon, fellow Australian and manager of the ice-cream kiosk, deserved another chance, and not just because he had eyes that made her stomach deep dive and a smile that made her heart race Olympic-fast.

Izzy looked at her watch then headed to the kiosk. When she arrived, the line was already snaking down the side of the boat. No sign of Deacon. That tick of approval wasn't happening any time soon. She joined the queue and waited for Deacon and her turn.

"What can I get you? No, let me guess." Deacon scrunched up his eyes. "Mango Madness. Double scoop." He gave a grin of satisfaction like he'd just pulled off a miracle, but his sarcasm wasn't earning him any customer service ticks.

Izzy watched Deacon labour with the scoop and awkwardly push it into the waffle cone. He handed her the ice-cream. "Have a great day." That smile again, the one that weakened her knees and her resolve.

She ate her ice-cream on a deckchair looking up at Fira, thinking about her plans for the evening and ways she could help Deacon turn that cross into a tick. Izzy finished her ice-cream, then went to change into something a little more glamorous, a little more Santorini.

മരു

Izzy stepped into one of the tenders ferrying passengers to the island and grabbed a seat. Deacon jumped on board just as it pulled away from the ship. His eyes scanned the boat and landed on Izzy. Her stomach flipped. Twice. Deacon came and stood in front of her. "Hey, M&M. How are you going?"

"M&M?"

"Mango Madness. Two scoops, waffle cone. You know, you really should branch out and try something different. So many flavours, so little time."

"And risk disappointment?"

"Take the risk. You might even like it." He looked around the boat. "Where's your friend?"

"Sarah had other plans." Izzy and Sarah were both travelling alone so they'd often catch up over meals and on excursions.

"Deacon. Over here," a crew member from the ship called out from the bow.

"Sorry. Gotta go."

Deacon had disappeared by the time she'd disembarked. Izzy headed toward the funicular, which looked like it would be quicker than a donkey and safer than the bus.

When she reached the peak, Izzy headed down the pedestrian way lined with art galleries, shops and restaurants. She was just about to go into a dress shop when she saw Sarah in the crowd ahead of her.

"Sarah?"

Sarah kept walking.

Izzy called out again and picked up her pace, but Sarah darted into a souvenir shop before she could catch her.

Izzy followed her inside. She wanted to ask Sarah to join her for dinner, but she was in the back corner, talking to a man. A couple of minutes later, Sarah disappeared behind a curtain. After ten minutes and strange looks from the shop assistant, Izzy decided to wait outside. She spent another ten minutes on the stone wall beside a life-sized puppet dressed in green, with gold shoes and a pout that would make Kim Kardashian jealous. If she waited much longer, she wouldn't have time to find a good vantage point to see the sunset.

By 8.00, Izzy had found the ideal restaurant; by 8.15, she was sipping a glass of chardonnay. She eyed the clear glass panel, the only thing standing between her and the four-hundred-metre drop, with the kind of suspicion she reserved for unsolicited phone calls. Izzy took another sip and tried to forget she was sitting on top of an extinct volcano. Loud voices and laughter caught her attention, but her eyes didn't leave the ball of fire slipping slowly into the sea. She had her priorities.

A laugh ripped through the restaurant, ruining the moment.

Sarah.

Izzy spun around and did a double take. Deacon had a girl on each arm, and Sarah was one of them. They joined a table of people she recognised as fellow passengers. No wonder Sarah had been so secretive. There were rules about staff fraternising with passengers. Izzy turned her back to them and enjoyed the last of the sunset.

A waiter appeared.

"Menu?" His smile was welcoming but his tone told her to eat or leave. He left her to make her choice and she was on the third page of the menu when she sensed a presence beside her.

"I'm still deciding."

"I can see that. Do you need any help?" She recognised the voice immediately and so did her stomach. She glanced up.

"Can I join you?"

Izzy glanced behind her, but Sarah and the rest of the group had disappeared. Her heart wanted to say yes, but the image of a big black cross on her evaluation form was like a ball of guilt wedged in her throat, trapping her words.

Deacon took her hesitation as an invitation to sit down. He waved to the waiter. "Would you like another drink?"

She recovered quickly.

"Just one." More than one would be fraternising, and then, there was the conflict of interest. She had to include him in her feedback.

"I thought you'd be with your friends."

He wanted to talk about her friends, but that was the last thing on her mind. The universe had opened a window of opportunity and she intended to jump through.

A musician had set up in the corner of the restaurant and was playing slow, getting-to-know-you music. Deacon talked about the Greek Islands and places he'd been. Izzy told him about working in her grandmother's antique shop, and her dreams of finishing her degree. The perfect segue. Izzy could see a big tick next to the ice-cream kiosk already.

"Do you like your job?"

"Love it."

Disbelief flickered across her face. "You sure?" This was going to be harder than she thought.

"Are you saying I don't?"

Izzy took a deep breath, tried a different approach. "Maybe ice-cream isn't your forté?" Her voice was tentative, careful of stepping on his self-esteem.

"Maybe you're right. What is my forté?" He leaned closer.

Izzy thought for a minute. Great body? Definitely. Great dancer? Probably. Great lover? Possibly. None of them were on the evaluation list. "Let me think about it."

"Why don't we go and find your friends, have a drink and some fun while you're thinking. I'll show you there's more to Fira than sunsets."

Izzy teetered on the edge of her decision like a cliff diver facing unfamiliar water. She wasn't really fraternising. Technically Deacon would be helping her to find her friends. She took a deep breath and stepped away from the cliff. "Thank you but I'll head back to the ship. Don't want it sailing without me."

"I'll walk you to the funicular."

She bought her ticket and they waited in line.

"So, you don't think I'm any good selling ice-cream?" A smile crept around the corners of his mouth.

"Well..."

"Take the tour of Knossos tomorrow morning. Maybe tour guiding is my forté."

The funicular was boarding.

"See you tomorrow." Deacon leaned down, his lips brushed her cheek and sent her pulse racing.

The buses arrived at Knossos early the next morning and the passengers were divided into smaller groups. Sarah grabbed Izzy's arm just as their group was moving,

"I'm going to get some water. I'll catch up." She pushed through the people behind them. Izzy looked around for Deacon, but he seemed to have disappeared as well.

The guide led them past columns, giant urns, dolphin murals and a peacock picking its way through the abandoned pieces of stone. Probably counting down the hours till the gates closed.

Their group was the last to get back to the buses. Sarah and Deacon were standing together, talking. Izzy joined them.

"I thought you were going to show me what a great a tour guide you are." She made her voice light and cheery to cover her disappointment.

"Another time. We'd better get back to the boat so you can get ready for the party tonight. The last night of a cruise is always a good one."

Sarah and Izzy ended up sitting together on the bus.

"Was Deacon in your group?" Izzy tried to keep her voice couldn't-care-less casual.

"No." Sarah leaned back against the seat and closed her eyes, shutting out the scenery and Izzy.

Izzy knocked on Sarah's door. The door swung open. Sarah was dressed but her hair was still wet.

"Won't be a minute."

Izzy sat on the side of the bed, her eyes flicking around the cabin, checking how it differed from hers. Bigger room, better view and a balcony the size of a football field. She glanced at the shelf under the mirror and saw a female figurine with snakes winding around its arms. She picked it up and admired it.

"Sarah — how fantastic! Where did you get this?"

Sarah poked her head around the corner of the bathroom. Shock flashed over her face followed by a fake smile and a fast recovery.

"I bought it at the shop when I went to get my water." Sarah snapped off the bathroom light, snatched the figurine and put it in the wardrobe. "C'mon, Let's have some fun."

Sarah had booked a table for eight so her new friends could join them. The couple opposite Izzy tried to include her in their conversation, but she was only interested in finding Deacon.

"Excuse me for a minute," Sarah interrupted their conversation. "I'll be back." Izzy frowned, wishing she had an excuse to escape as well.

"Izzy?"

Deacon. Her heart slipped and skidded. She turned around.

"Would you like to dance?" He held out his hand and she grabbed it like a lifeline.

She stood and faced him. "Are you allowed to dance with the passengers?" She lowered her voice so no-one else could hear.

"I'll risk it." He slipped his arm around her waist and led her to the dancefloor. They faced each other and Deacon pulled her close. She felt his breath on her neck, his heart thumping. She couldn't do this. The evaluation form was due tomorrow. Izzy pushed against him. He loosened his hold, looked into her eyes for an answer.

"You want to sit down?" His tone was confused and unsure.

"Yes, um, no. I don't know. I need to speak to you."

He looked at his watch. "We could meet on the upper deck in an hour. I'll be off duty then, and we can talk without interruption."

"That would be fantastic."

Deacon led her back to the table then walked away.

An hour later, Izzy headed to the elevator. A hand grabbed her from behind and pulled her around.

"Sarah." Izzy pulled her arm away. "What's wrong?"

"Where's the figurine?" Sarah stood in front of her, feet apart and hands on her hips.

"The Snake Lady?"

"Give it back." Sarah screwed up her face and spat out her words.

"I haven't got it. And I can't believe you'd believe I'd steal it." Izzy's voice stood its ground even though her body wanted to retreat.

"Give it back. Now."

Izzy stepped back. "You need to tell security, not go around making false accusations." She turned and took the elevator to the upper deck to meet Deacon.

He was leaning against the railing, waiting. "Everything okay?"

"Sarah accused me of stealing her figurine, but that's not why I wanted to talk."

"What's on your mind?"

"I— uh— I haven't been totally honest with you."

"If you're talking about my future in ice-cream, I think you've been more than honest."

"This is serious."

"Okay." He stepped away, his back against the railing of the ship, his arms folded. "What do you want to tell me?"

"I'm scared you could lose your job. And it'll be my fault." Izzy's words fell over each other in their rush to be heard.

Deacon took both of Izzy's hands. "Slow down. What are you talking about?"

She looked over her shoulder, lowered her voice. "I'm a mystery shopper."

"What's a mystery shopper?"

"Someone paid to give feedback about products and services."

Two furrows deepened between his eyes, then his expression lit up like someone putting the final piece in a jigsaw puzzle.

"You're gonna give me a bad evaluation?"

"Deacon, I can't lie — I just don't think ice-cream is your forté. I'm sorry."

"Don't be." He took her hands and squeezed them. "I have to go now, but we can talk about this later." Deacon was supposed to be off duty, but he was clearly upset by what she'd said. He'd raced off and left her alone with a full moon, the sounds of 'Auld Lang Syne' and regrets about a lost opportunity.

CRNO

It was the last day on the cruise. Time to say goodbye to Greece. Time to say goodbye to Deacon. She'd been looking for him all day to finish their talk but hadn't had any luck. She'd looked everywhere, except the ice-cream kiosk. Izzy went there hoping to see him one more time.

Brendan. Busy refilling the empty ice-cream containers.

Her hopes joined her heart in the pit of her stomach. Ice-cream was a poor consolation prize, but it was all she had. Izzy looked at the selection. "I'll have mango…" Izzy thought of Deacon and decided he was right. Time to take a risk and try something different. "No, make that a Pistachio Passion."

"Sorry, no pistachio today."

"But I just saw you put in a new tub."

The line of people behind her was getting longer and louder. Brendan had no choice. He slid the lid off the tub and picked up a single cone.

"Double please."

He looked from Izzy to the tub, replaced the single cone with a double, scraped some ice-cream into it and held it out to Izzy.

Izzy left his hand and the ice-cream hanging in mid-air. Her expression told him to try again.

Brendan scraped some more ice-cream from the tub, exposing the top of a statue. Brendan saw it at the same time. Tried to scrape the ice-cream over it. Tried to cover it.

Sarah's figurine.

Brendan handed her the ice-cream and put the lid back on the tub.

"Thank you, I'm going to enjoy this." Izzy's words camouflaged her surprise. She had to find Sarah and clear her name. She turned a corner and collided with Deacon. He gripped her arms to stop her from falling.

"Good morning, Izzy. Get your report in?" His eyes took in her ice-cream, and he gave her a lop-sided smile. "I see you're living dangerously."

"Brendan…"

"Not up to standard? Not surprised."

"He's stolen Sarah's figurine. It's in the pistachio ice-cream."

She was expecting him to laugh at her, make fun of her, tell her she was imagining things. But he didn't. "Leave it with me."

Izzy went straight to Sarah's room to tell her about the figurine, but there were no happy smiles and no apology.

૭૪૪૭

Izzy stood on the rooftop bar, gazing at the Acropolis above her bathed in the golden light. Tomorrow she'd be on a flight to Australia with a heavy suitcase and a heavy heart. Sarah and her friends were enjoying each other's company at the far end of the rooftop and had left her alone.

Noise exploded through the door onto the rooftop. Six men in blue uniforms walked straight up to Sarah. Deacon wasn't far behind. He paused at the door, scanned the rooftop, and headed toward Izzy.

"What're you doing here?"

Her voice was full of surprise, her heart full of hope.

"Making sure you don't get caught up in all this." He nodded toward the police herding Sarah and her friends down the stairs.

"What's happening?"

"Your friend Sarah is being arrested for trafficking in antiquities."

"How do you know that?"

"Izzy, I haven't been totally honest with you either." His voice softened, stumbling its way to the truth. "I don't work for the cruise company."

Izzy's eyes opened as wide as her mouth.

"I'm working with a multi-national task force tracking down stolen antiquities."

"Why didn't you tell me?"

His voice dropped guilty-low. "It wasn't until yesterday I realised you weren't part of the gang. When you told me about Brendan stealing Sarah's figurine, I knew you weren't involved. Brendan was Sarah's contact, but it turns out he decided to go it alone."

"I don't understand why he'd try and hide something so valuable in ice-cream. It doesn't make sense."

"That's why he arranged to replace me at the kiosk. I guess he thought putting it in a tub of ice-cream was the one way he could keep an eye on it. Apparently Pistachio Passion isn't that popular. We're very lucky you chose it."

"I followed your advice about taking a risk."

"Speaking of taking risks, how would you like to have dinner with me?"

"Even though I gave you bad feedback?"

"*Because* you gave me bad feedback." Deacon took her hand. Electricity shot up her arm and straight to her heart like a lightning bolt hitting a tree. Izzy wanted to feel his arms wrap around her, feel his heartbeat against hers, feel his skin on her skin. Their lips met, gently, lovingly, deeply.

Izzy pulled away slightly.

"Something wrong?"

"Nothing wrong. I think I may have just found your forté."

15

MELT ME

JILLIAN JONES

Joshua Taylor spied the ice cream shop across the street at the same time as his sister did. Amber lifted her arm. "Ugh." If there was one thing she lived for, it was ice cream. He rolled her wheelchair closer.

The facade, reminiscent of a Brighton Beach box, had faux ice cream cones as tall as him, adorning each side of the entrance. But it was a clothing store. What were the chances?

"Wanna go in?" Amber nodded and, without hesitation, he wheeled her in.

He couldn't suppress the grimace. Soft pink walls fitted the theme and kitsch ice cream cone decals adorned plinths and wall panels. Succulents, of all things, sat in the window display and atop several other surfaces, potted in petite ceramic planters which took inspiration from an ice cream cone.

"Ice Cream Fashion," he read aloud, from the Golden Gaytime coloured neon sign on the back wall. "Weird name for a clothing shop."

"It's a play on 'I scream fashion'," said a young blonde, appearing from behind a rack of colourful dresses. He placed her as mid-twenties with nice curves beneath her yellow sundress. Her nametag said 'Sam'. The saccharine smile on her face matched the décor. "But, it's called ice cream because we're taste makers in fashion, creating cool and addictively sweet fashion for our fabulous customers." His usually disinterested heart fluttered when she flashed a dazzling smile at him. He dismissed the sensation.

"Interesting concept." He sent her a tight smile, but her gaze was already on his sister. "We're after a dress for her twenty-first. Can you help us?" Several attempts by her carer had failed. Now it was his turn.

"Of course," Sam chirped. The smile stayed in place as she made eye contact with Amber. "And what's your name?" A twinge of respect swirled through his gut.

"Em ba," his sister mumbled.

"Amber," he clarified.

"What a lovely name. I'm Sam. Let's find an amazing dress for you." The assistant's smile broadened as she spoke. That she was bothering made a pleasant change from the stuffy sales assistants who wouldn't normally give them a second glance.

"No dwess. I weem." His sister spoke loud enough to turn heads.

"Oh." The smile fell from chirpy Sam's face as she dropped to her knees in front of Amber. "Did you think this was an ice cream parlour?"

"Affirmative." Joshua sighed as his sister burst into tears, shifting in her chair. That, and the way she was wringing her hands indicated she was becoming distressed. "Time to abort," he mumbled to himself. He needed to find somewhere to buy ice cream. "She's not fond of shopping," he explained, reversing the wheelchair away from the crouching woman. She tilted her chin towards him, revealing cleavage he hadn't noticed before, and his stomach tightened.

"And you thought a clothing shop named ice cream might entice her?" She gaped, but grabbed the arm of the chair, halting Joshua's escape, as Amber sobbed louder.

"I apologise for the inconvenience," Joshua offered, his primary goal now to exit the store. The pretty blonde returned her attention to him. Her gaze, a stunning clear sky-blue, meshed with his, knocking all the air from his lungs. "I need to get out of here. Get Amber some ice cream before she screams the shop down," he added.

Thankfully, Sam stood, her gaze softening, a slight furrow appearing between her brows.

"Wait there. I might be able to help." She disappeared behind a door featuring a neon icy pole sign and reappeared a moment later, holding a real ice cream: a cornetto with swirling pink and blue dollops on the top. Amber's sobs subsided.

"Do you entice all customers with these?" He raised one eyebrow at the sales assistant.

"Only our VIPs." She handed the decadent treat to Amber, who took it without hesitation. "Just did some grocery shopping," Sam added, addressing Joshua.

"May I wheel you around?" Sam asked Amber, hands on knees as she leaned in, making eye contact. Amber nodded.

A lap around the store ended with Amber selecting a pretty mustard-coloured dress printed with small white flowers. The knee-length flared skirt was fine; it was the form fitting bodice and cinched waist that made him wince. Couldn't Sam see it wouldn't fit Amber?

"This will be better." He held up a kaftan-style dress that he'd noticed during their circumnavigation.

"What's wrong with the one Amber's chosen?" Sam blinked. Looking from the kaftan dress back to Joshua.

"Isn't it obvious?" He gestured at his sister. "Amber is hardly a standard size eight. She has a brace around her torso and…"

"I know." Sam interrupted, retrieving a tape measure from the pink-and-white-striped ice cream cart sales counter. "Made to Amber's measurements, it'll look amazing."

"What? The party is next week!"

Sam didn't meet his gaze, just smiled at Amber. "Mind if I take your measurements?" Amber granted permission with a tilt of her head, and Sam swiftly and expertly took his sister's measurements. He'd never seen a woman interact with his kid sister like this. "I promise it'll be ready on time." Sam stood and faced him, her clear blue gaze mesmerising him once more.

"Is this a standard service?" It seemed unusual for an off-the-rack clothing store.

"No." She smiled. She was being kind, and it sent his brain a little fuzzy.

"Can I expect to see you when I collect it?" he blurted but wished he hadn't. What was his problem? He didn't date.

"Sounds like you're angling for a date." She chuckled. He frowned, perturbed by her kindness and beauty. "I was kidding." She raised an eyebrow at him before turning to Amber. "I think you need a new carer. This one has no sense of humour."

"I'm not her carer," he snapped. Where had that reaction come from? She glared, rightly so. "I'm her brother," he added, in a gentler tone.

"Right." Her gaze softened before it returned to his sister. "Guess you're stuck with him." Sam raised one quizzical eyebrow at Amber and the corner of Amber's mouth twitched. A rare attempt at a smile.

"I meant to say, is it necessary that we see you to collect the dress?" That still didn't sound right. It was like he was tongue-tied.

"It'll be waiting for collection at the front counter." She rolled her eyes.

"Hang on. Is this the price?" he said, checking the price tag on the dress hanging on the back of Amber's wheelchair. "That's obscene for a mass-produced item manufactured in China." He cocked his eyebrow, knowing he was right. "Goodness knows what you're going to charge for a custom-made one of these."

"Same price," Sam said with a frown, folding her arms under her breasts. He dropped his gaze to avoid staring as heat infused his face. What was his problem?

"They're made here in Australia," she added, sending him a warm smile. "If I could have your name and number, we'll call when it's ready. You can pay on collection."

As she accepted his business card, he sensed the blood drain from his face. She was the most beautiful woman he'd ever seen and incredibly accepting of his sister, but he refused to be tempted. He couldn't afford such a distraction ever again.

"Lawyer, hey?" She read his card, her expression inscrutable. "That explains it."

"Explains what?" He should've remained silent.

"So serious." She put his card in her pocket.

"Because I'm responsible rather than frivolous?" He just couldn't keep his mouth shut.

"Have a fun party, Amber." She presented her bedazzling smile to his sister but didn't share it with him or meet his gaze again before he wheeled Amber from the store. For some reason, he sensed a deep level of disappointment that had nothing to do with the price of the dress.

Joshua couldn't keep his mind from wandering. Mostly thoughts of Sam, the shop assistant. By lunchtime the following day, he gave in and returned to the shop to apologise for his behaviour.

"May I help you?" A different sales assistant greeted him. Her name tag said 'Ella'.

"I was hoping to speak to Sam." He couldn't see her anywhere.

"She's not expected today. Can I assist?"

"When is she next rostered on?"

"She's not." Ella blinked, surprised.

"She took an order for a dress yesterday, though she said it was not something you usually do. Can you check it'll be filled?"

"Sam's the owner." The girl laughed.

"Right." Unexpected. Sam seemed so young.

Ella nodded. "She only comes in occasionally, but your order is safe. If you want to change anything, I can message her." Her plastic and polite smile so unlike Sam's warm smile yesterday.

"No. Thank you," he said, turning to leave, his gut churning. He hadn't been himself yesterday. "Have a good day," he added as an afterthought, glancing over his shoulder, but Ella had already shifted her attention, greeting a customer.

"Hot but gruff and rude." Samantha Davies laughed as she read Ella's text message. She had her suspicions about who it might be. And he might appear gruff and rude, but she could see how much he cared for his sister. He had a soft centre "With a gaze and voice that might just melt me," she said aloud to no-one. Retrieving the business card taped to the order page with Amber's measurements, she keyed in Joshua Taylor's mobile number.

Greeted by his messaging service, she replied, "It's Sam, from Ice Cream Fashion. I'm told you called into the shop. If you require changes to Amber's dress, please let me know ASAP."

The dress was well underway. Any changes would slow things down.

Not wanting to miss his call, she added his information as a new contact. Thankfully, she only had to wait five minutes before his incoming call flashed on her screen.

"What changes do you want?" She didn't bother with formalities, not with him.

"I'm calling to apologise for my behaviour yesterday and thank you for what you did for Amber." His voice, smooth like soft velvet, set off a tingle in her belly, as it had done yesterday.

"Okay," she managed.

"When the dress is ready, perhaps I could collect it over dinner." Had she heard correctly? "Sam? Are you there?"

"I'm here." She sucked in a breath, butterflies fluttering in her belly. "Are you asking me out?"

"I guess I am." His soft chuckle sent feathery sensations through her whole body.

"Umm." She hesitated. Was this a bad idea? "Sure."

Two days later, sitting across a small table from the man, Sam found herself entranced by the upward curve of Joshua's mouth. In a relaxed mood, he was by far the most attractive man she'd ever met. She struggled to shift her gaze from his lips when he smiled. The light-coloured flower-patterned shirt beneath his dark business suit seemed almost playful. Her heart softened towards him. She was seeing a different side to him, one that hadn't been obvious when he visited her store.

"How did you come to own a dress shop?" he asked.

"Mum taught me to sew, and when I finished high school, I studied fashion while working part-time to get some sales experience," she explained. "When I graduated, my father financed a clothing factory and retail store, so I'm the first to admit how fortunate I am. Working my dream job. I have a team for the manufacturing side, but I keep my skills up by making several dresses each month and donating them to a women's shelter where my mother volunteers. It's a small token, but I love how it makes them feel special."

છ૪ળ

Though his gaze savoured her full luscious lips as she spoke, even the obvious beauty of his dinner date paled against her inner warmth and kindness.

"I count my blessings every day," she said. He'd never seen eyes so clear and honest.

"That's admirable." He'd met no-one quite like her. She sparkled with a love of life. What he would give to bathe in her sunshine a little longer. "Your father may have funded your business, but it sounds like your efforts have made it a success. You should be proud of all you've achieved and that, even better, you're a beacon of love and kindness in the world," he added. She blushed and his heart fluttered. Was that a tiny shimmer of possibility infiltrating his barricaded heart? Could a relationship with this woman be worth the risk?

"What about you? What made you go into law?" she asked, before taking a sip of sparkling water.

He sucked in a deep breath. "Ten years ago, a car ran a red light and mowed down my family as they crossed the road. Both my parents were killed and Amber ended up with a broken spine and brain damage. She was in a coma for several weeks. Before the accident, she was a healthy eleven-year-old."

Sam gaped. "Oh, I'm so sorry." He shook his head, waving away her concern. Sympathy didn't bring his family back. "How old were you?"

"Sixteen."

"You would've had to grow up fast." She chewed her bottom lip. He swallowed, hard.

"We were shunted between well-meaning relatives with Amber often placed in respite care, until I could afford to move us back to the family home and manage her care myself."

"She's lucky to have you."

He shrugged. "I'm not so sure. If I hadn't been lagging so far behind, distracted — I was chatting up a girl — I might have saved them. I noticed the car too late; I was too far away for them to hear me yell. A hit and run, and with no camera at the traffic lights, the driver got away with it." He sucked in a breath. "Anyway, I've made it my mission to fight for the rights of others in similar situations." He'd worked hard and, at twenty-six, was an in-demand barrister, ambitious and motivated, but not fulfilled. Sitting with this warm, wonderful woman made him re-evaluate his situation.

"My heart is icy. I'm not all that kind." He sent her a weak smile.

"I'm not so sure about that. When I mentioned your name, my mother said she knew you, that you do *pro bono* to support women in the shelter where she volunteers. And you care for Amber at home when it would be easier and more convenient to place her in respite care. That's a huge kindness."

He shrugged. "She has a carer most of the time. My grandma Tess is looking after her right now."

A loud ping from his mobile interrupted the conversation — a message from his grandmother. His heart sank as he read it. It was a sign. He shouldn't have let Sam distract him. He should have been there looking after Amber.

"Amber's just been admitted to hospital with fluid in her lungs. I've gotta go." Joshua stood. His vision beginning to blur, he could barely see Sam. He made for the exit, tossing a one-hundred dollar note at the man behind the front counter to pay for their meal, before rushing to be by Amber's side. The last time a girl distracted him, disaster struck. He couldn't allow that again.

જાછ

Sam entered the hospital room to find Amber sleeping peacefully, Joshua seated on one side of her bed, and an elderly lady on the other.

It hadn't escaped her awareness how triggered Joshua had been the previous evening, about being on a date when Amber experienced a health crisis.

"You forgot the dress." Sam held up the garment bag and Joshua startled.

"Thanks, but you didn't have to." He accepted the item and draped it over the chair he was sitting on.

Sam leaned over, taking a closer look at Amber. Her colour seemed good, and she was breathing effortlessly, with no gurgling sounds.

"Get well, beautiful girl. Your party is in three days. I want to see you in this dress. I can even come braid your hair and do your make-up."

"She can't hear." Joshua said, his tone flat.

"How do you know?" Sam frowned.

"I'm Tess." The older woman interrupted, offering her hand.

"Sam."

She nodded. "He's a bit tetchy. Might need a coffee. Would you mind accompanying him?"

"Sure," Sam replied, a fluttery feeling in her belly at the thought of being alone with Joshua again.

Joshua grumbled as his grandmother shooed them from the room.

"The rugged, unshaven look is sexy on you," Sam teased as they stood by the vending machine, disposable coffee cups in hand. He sent her a weak smile.

"Listen, Sam. I'm sorry, but I can't see you again." He stared intently at his cup, then turned to leave.

"Why?" She stepped closer, blocking his path.

"Don't you see. It's a sign." He glanced at her briefly before casting his gaze in the direction of Amber's room. "I go on a date and my sister ends up in hospital."

"You seriously believe that you're not allowed to have some fun?" No response. "I don't believe your parents or Amber would agree," Sam offered. "Imagine what might have happened if you hadn't been lagging behind, chatting up that girl. Amber could have been left all alone." She inched closer and lifted a hand to his cheek.

"I've never thought about it like that." His fatigue-ridden gaze made her heart ache for him. And yet he seemed to stand a little taller.

"My intuition tells me Amber will be fine for her birthday party," Sam said.

"I hope so," Joshua replied, edging so close his breath brushed her lips. When his gaze landed on her mouth, heat rushed through her entire body. "Will you join us?"

She managed a nod. "What about another date?" he whispered, and Sam's belly did a flip as his thumb touched her chin.

"Sure." She sighed before their lips met.

16

SWEETER THAN ICE CREAM

DENISE ASTON

Daniel Hollier pulled his security belt from the back of the truck and clipped it around his waist. Lifting the cooler that he'd brought with him from the truck, he grinned as he walked to the rear of the building. In three minutes, he'd see Sarah.

Excitement and a healthy dose of nerves knotted his stomach. Today was the day he was going to get Sarah Midas to notice him. Hell, not just notice him; today, if things went well, Sarah was going to speak with him and he was going to ask her out.

The elevator pinged, announcing his arrival on level 23. He stepped out and stopped for a second to admire the view. Lights twinkled across the expanse of water, giving the city a magical quality that it lacked during the day. It differed greatly from his home town, but was no less beautiful. It just wasn't home, the Valley was, and if it wasn't for his sister and his niece, and now his attraction to Sarah, he'd have returned home months ago.

Sarah's voice came from down the hallway, cutting into his thoughts. His eyes closed, and he stood still. A half smile lifted his lips. That voice of hers had the power to draw him in. He moved closer to her office, her words coming to him in snatches. *She sounds annoyed.* He frowned. His large hands clenched at his sides as he strode quickly toward her open office door, thankful everyone else had left for the day and he wouldn't be caught eavesdropping.

"I don't know how you think that's fair. We agreed that we'd launch the new line in eight weeks, not four." Her voice pitched higher as she added, "I understand the financial situation. I understand it better than you do, but a deal is a deal and you have no right to change the timeline without giving me more notice."

Daniel heard her fingers tap on her desk. He should walk away. Listening in to a private phone conversation was poor form. He turned to leave but stopped when he heard her say, "I'll agree, Jerome, provided you drop the interest rate you're charging." Silence, and then in a harsh tone he'd never heard her use before, she added, "Okay, you have a deal. Send it through in writing." More silence, then her voice broke as she shouted, "No. I *don't* trust you." He heard her phone clatter to the surface of her desk, then her chair squeaked.

Not wanting to be caught snooping, he moved to continue past her office. Her much smaller body slammed into his. The cooler slipped. He tightened his grip on it even as his other hand shot out to steady her as she teetered on the impossibly high-heeled shoes she favoured. He looked down into her upturned face and, just like always, the words he'd thought about saying to her dried up.

Green eyes, the colour of moss beside a deep forest pool, blinked up at him. Thick black lashes lifted and fell. Her lips moved, but for a second he didn't register her words, just the lush shape of her mouth. His hand was still on her arm and he slowly let it drift down to encircle her wrist. He knew he needed to let go, but it was difficult not to want to savour the moment. Six months he'd waited for Sarah to notice him. Still, if he didn't put a bit of distance between them, he'd continue to act like a complete idiot. Heat crawled up his neck as her smile stretched wider, as if she knew what he was thinking.

✿

Sweet mother of mercy, Daniel's touching me. Sarah knew the right thing to do was to step back, but she couldn't bring herself to pull away. His hand on her wrist catapulted her into a fantasy world where Daniel finally saw her. She exhaled. She'd wanted him to notice her for months, and yet he always seemed to look straight through her.

Not tonight, though. Tonight, his brown eyes, the colour of dark bitter chocolate, stared down at her like he was finally seeing her. She flicked her hair over her shoulder and smiled with satisfaction as he tracked the movement. She took in the security guard's dark blue uniform stretching across his broad shoulders and the ink she could see peeking out from under the short sleeves. The way he moved, the way he looked; all of it screamed 'protector'. She desperately needed someone like him in her life because of the stupid decision she'd made to borrow money from Jerome, a man with no scruples, and ties to the local bikie gang.

Shoving away unpleasant thoughts of Jerome, Sarah stayed where she was. She was desperate to speak with Daniel instead of watching him like some crazy woman. She inhaled, trying to calm her racing heart, but instead her dazed brain caught the sugary-sweet, creamy smell that clung to his body.

"Why do you smell like ice cream?" Her hand popped up to cover her mouth. "That was rude." She shook her head to clear it. "Not that ice cream is a bad smell. I mean, I smell ice cream and all I can think about is eating it."

Daniel's eyebrows rose, and he chuckled.

Her eyes widened. *Ohmigod could I be any more obvious?* She rushed into nervous speech.

"No. Not eating. I meant to say licking." She stepped back as more words tumbled out. "I don't mean licking or eating you..." Her voice trailed off. "I'm going to stop talking."

His eyes sparkled as he teased, "Do I make you nervous, Sarah?"

She blushed. Standing up straighter, she crossed her fingers behind her back. "No, you do not".

Although I do spend way too much time thinking about you and me getting together when I should be working.

"Hmmm." Daniel side-eyed her, clearly unconvinced. "I smell like ice cream because I was making it before I came here."

Her eyebrows squished together. "You work at an ice cream parlour and security?"

"No. I made it because you like ice cream." He cleared his throat. "I overheard you talking to one of your people about how ice cream is your kryptonite."

Her mouth dropped open. "You made ice cream for me?"

"Well," he laughed, reaching up and rubbing the back of his neck, "I tried to." He lifted the cooler in his hand higher, so it was in her line of sight. "You want to try it?"

She glanced up at him through her lashes. Her heart thumped harder.

"Yes, please."

He brushed past her into her office and placed the cooler down on her desk. The muscles in his arms flexed as he lifted the lid then dug into the frozen contents nestled inside. Holding the spoon out toward her, his heavy-lidded stare held hers as she boldly wrapped her hand over his, guiding it to her mouth.

Her eyes drifted shut at the feel of his warm, strong hand and, as the cold creamy texture hit her tongue, she groaned.

"Oh, that's goooood. Toffee is my favourite flavour."

Her eyes opened as she heard him laugh softly. Fascinated, she watched the muscles in his neck tighten as he visibly swallowed, staring at her lips. The delicious smell of him wafted over her. She swayed closer, inhaling deeply, letting the sweet sugary scent tease her senses.

He clenched his jaw, his eyes still locked on her lips.

She leaned in further, only to jerk back a step as she heard a door slam in the distance and then the elevator pinged. She frowned. *Who on earth would come back to the office at this time of night? And why was someone accessing the stairwell when the elevator was working?*

"You expecting anyone?"

"No, but it has to be someone from my team because no-one else has after-hours access."

"Your employees usually come back this late?" Daniel's voice was gruff.

Sarah shook her head.

"Wait here," he growled.

She hovered behind her desk for several seconds after Daniel left, before deciding that being trapped there wasn't smart. Slowly, she edged out into the hallway, stopping to listen. Someone shouted. She heard a thud. Was it Daniel? Was he hurt? Quietly, she moved back into her office and slid her desk drawer open, pulling her gun out. Ever since she'd done the deal with Jerome Perez to bankroll her jewellery launch, she'd kept it close in case one of Jerome's associates paid her a visit.

She could hear someone running toward her, their ragged breathing sounding desperate. She ducked into the supply room and quietly angled the door so her body was hidden behind it, but she could still see out. A woman dashed past with a man thundering down the corridor not too far behind her. The woman looked terrified. The man looked angry enough to kill. *What the hell is going on?*

They disappeared through the door at the far end of the hall.

Move now. Sarah stepped out of her heeled shoes and hurried toward the elevator. She rounded the corner and spotted Daniel's crumpled body lying on the floor. Blood pooled around his head, darkening his blue security uniform. She ran to him.

Be okay, be okay. Her brain kicked off the chant as she knelt, swallowing the bile in her mouth, checking to see that he was still breathing. As his breath tickled her cheek, she exhaled the breath she'd been holding.

I need to get help. No, stop the bleeding first. Nausea twisted in her stomach even as she pushed herself to her feet and ran back down the hallway to the staff room. She tugged the medical kit from the top of the fridge and ran back to Daniel, swiping her phone from her desk as she ran by her office.

Puffing heavily, she dropped the kit beside him and found a bandage. Blowing air from her lungs, she took a deep breath and pressed the bandage to the wound. With one hand holding the bandage firmly in place, she called emergency services and got an ambulance on its way.

Please wake up. She wished she could rewind the clock and go back thirty minutes and have Daniel just arriving into her office and offering her his homemade ice cream.

His eyes fluttered open and his hand moved up to cover hers on his head. He slow-blinked at her. She had the sudden urge to pull him to her and tell him he was going to be okay.

Instead, she muttered, "What happened?"

"A woman came bolting out of the stairwell. Then the lift doors opened and a guy tried to push past me to get to her. I grabbed his arm and he pistol-whipped me."

Sarah glanced back down the hallway. "Should I call... "

Daniel squeezed her hand. "Don't worry. I called it in before I passed out. My brothers will make sure the woman's safe."

"You have brothers?"

"One, but I also ride with a motorcycle club, so only one of the brothers I'm talking about is blood-related. They should be here soon." Daniel pulled himself into a sitting position, grimacing as he moved.

Sarah searched for a topic to distract him, praying the ambulance would arrive soon. "I loved the ice cream. It was sweet of you to make it for me."

"Loved it enough to go on a date with me?" He wiggled his eyebrows.

"You're white as a sheet with blood everywhere and you're asking me out on a date?"

"Been trying to ask you out for months. Seems like I might've had some sense knocked into me." He tried to stand up, but Sarah shook her head, placing a gentle hand on his chest. He stilled immediately, grinning up into her concerned face. "Had much worse than this, Sarah. Now you gonna answer my question?"

Sarah hesitated. "I'm not sure I can. People are depending on me."

"I know that feeling." She quirked an eyebrow, hoping he'd continue to share. His gaze dropped to the floor as he murmured, "I'm helping my sister out."

She knew it was more than that. She'd overhead a conversation between him and his sister months earlier. From the one-sided conversation, she'd figured out he was protecting his sister and niece from his sister's ex. His willingness to put his life on hold for family had turned his good looks into something much more attractive.

His voice was determined as he added, "You've got to eat, right?"

She smiled at his persistence. "Yes."

Daniel snapped his fingers. "I'll bring us a picnic that we can have in the office. Tomorrow night suit you?"

Sarah laughed. "I think you might need to give it a couple of days to get over your head injury. But when you're ready, text me the time and day and tell me what to bring."

"You're all I need." His voice was husky and just as his eyes dropped to her lips again, the elevator pinged announcing they had company. It was too soon for the ambulance to have arrived. She reached for her gun as Daniel's hand closed over hers. "It's okay. It'll be my brothers coming for me. Ignore them." Sure enough, the lift doors opened to reveal three burly men inside. Ignoring them, Daniel's intent stare remained locked on her.

"You got anything you don't like to eat?"

"No. I'm easy." A moment too late, she realised what she'd implied. Heat crawled up her neck.

Daniel's eyebrows raised and a mischievous gleam appeared in his eyes. "Easy, huh?" he teased.

"I just meant I'm easy to please." Sarah's eyes widened. *I need to stop talking. I'm making it worse.*

"Really?" Daniel drawled.

She needed to focus, retrieve the situation, not act like a flustered teenager. "I'm happy to eat anything you feed me."

Darn it, that sounded even worse.

Daniel's smile stretched wider.

She could pull this back. Her hands went to her hips, and she ground out, "Dessert's on me."

Daniel chuckled as she threw her hands in the air and huffed, "Oh, come on."

The young man standing closest to her let out a loud guffaw of laughter. She turned a fierce look on him. He bit his lip so hard she thought he might draw blood. The other man stared hard at the wall, not making eye contact, and the third man didn't even try to hide his grin. Ignoring their amused expressions, she bit out, "Ambulance should be here any minute."

The younger man, who looked a lot like Daniel, grunted. When she turned her glare back on him, he smirked at her. When she held his stare, he laughed. "No need for an ambulance, Spitfire, we got our own Doc."

The tallest of the three men crouched down beside her, muttering, "You should leave."

She raised her eyebrows.

Daniel squeezed her hand. "He's right. That man and woman weren't here for you, but I'd feel better if you let Axel walk you to your car." He must've seen her expression because he squeezed her hand. "I know he looks scary, but you can trust him."

Axel made a noise that sounded suspiciously like a snort, then he turned on his heel and headed over to the elevator. She assumed that was her cue to leave with him. With one last look at Daniel, she stood up. "I need to collect my things," she said, already turning toward her office. Her days of dancing to a man's tune were behind her, or at least they would be once she got Jerome out of her life.

Daniel texted and called her over the next seven days. Even though she was frantic at work, his calls were the highlight of her day. She learned so much about him; she was already halfway out the door toward falling in love. And then yesterday he'd said he would bring a picnic into the office for them to share. He'd insisted too that she didn't need to bring anything, that he had the whole thing organised.

She'd readily agreed to the date, then spent the night worrying about what to wear.

When seven p.m. finally arrived the next day, she stood up from behind her desk and smoothed her dress down. Walking out into the hallway she covered the short distance down toward the elevator. It pinged and Daniel stepped out. Sarah stood still, temporarily stunned into silence.

Daniel wore a suit that fitted his body like a second skin, accentuating his muscled arms and making his broad shoulders look even wider. His dark brown eyes looked even darker against the charcoal of the suit and his lilac shirt. She inhaled deeply and grinned as she saw his cooler peeking out of the hamper he held. She could guess what he had planned for dessert.

Her stomach flip-flopped at the bunch of roses he held in his other hand. He caught sight of her and his awestruck expression made the effort she'd taken with her appearance well worth the time she'd spent. He moved over to her and leaned in to kiss her cheek. "You smell divine," he murmured, his warm breath caressing her ear, causing her to shiver.

She brushed the side of his cheek with her hand and made a show of sniffing his neck. "You too. I'm guessing ice cream for dessert?"

He nodded. Smirking, he added, "I tried a new flavour this time."

"You did?"

"Yep. I call it, *Kiss me, please.*"

Sarah grinned. "I'd like to try that."

"Yeah?" His eyebrow lifted as he stepped toward her.

Sarah tilted her face up and as Daniel's lips brushed hers in a tender caress, Sarah realised while ice cream might taste sweet, Daniel's lips were even sweeter.

SPICY BITES

Want to try something a little spicier?

Why not try our Spicy Bites Anthology?

SPICY BITES 2022:

MACHINES

Spicy Bites anthologies can be purchased from the
Romance Writers of Australia store

http://romanceaustralia.com/shop/

COMING IN **2023**

Sweet Treats

Think of all those yummy treats that make you feel good, or that you might get or make for your loved ones.

The theme for 2023 is

Lollipops

Find full details on the Romance Writers of Australia website

https://romanceaustralia.com/contests-overview/sweet-treats-anthology/

Previous Little Gems and Sweet Treats anthologies can be purchased from the Romance Writers of Australia store

https://romanceaustralia.com/shop/

ABOUT THE AUTHORS

Alison Middleton

Alison Middleton is a writer of contemporary romance and other things.

Originally from Scotland, she has somehow managed to stay in Australia. She is a self-confessed massive nerd who enjoys reading, being snarky, and spending too much money on wine and books.

Follow Alison on Instagram at @alimiddleton8.

Jacinta Peachey

For years, *Jacinta Peachey* has lied about her age whilst travelling the world, refusing to grow up. After running a dental practice for fifteen years, she retired and has time to write. Now reading is research, not a guilty pleasure.

With a 'do as I say not as I do' attitude, coffee, red wine, and chocolate fuel her writing passion. Her stories focus on strong, independent, yet mixed-up women as they navigate life's unexpected turns.

Jacinta lives in Perth with her husband, a reluctant muse, and Eddie, a terrier who is surprisingly good at editing, waiting impatiently to travel again.

Sue-Ellen Pashley

A writer of copious words – because if they didn't come out, she's sure her head would explode – Sue-Ellen has ten published stories: *Aquila*, *When Henry Met Gina*, *The Jade Goddess*, *Streamer*, *The Flight*, *Talon Marked*, *The Rise*, *Blue*, *Booked for Murder* and *Sphenurus*. Her children's picture book - *The Jacket*, was released in Australia, UK, US and Korea.

Sue-Ellen lives in Queensland with her family, dogs and a snake called Slide. She loves quirky shoes, dark chocolate and good tea. An eternal optimist, she enjoys making things difficult for her protagonists but loves a satisfying ending.

www.sueellenpashley.com

https://www.facebook.com/sueellenpashleyauthor

Instagram – sueellenpashleyauthor

Bridget W Deen

Bridget W Deen is a Sydney born writer with a deep love of books filled with fantasy and romance. Having graduated from university with a Bachelor of Musical Theatre and a Grad Dip in Secondary Education, Bridget spent years performing, teaching and reading, until a new found love of writing stole all of her attention. Currently she is working on two novels with the goal to publish them in the near future. Messaging strangers about books is her favourite past time and she loves doing it through her instagram @bwdbooks or through her website bridgetwdeen.com

Fiona M Marsden

Fiona M Marsden started as an avid reader. She was late in finding romance novels, but once found, they became an addiction. Considering she wrote poetry and stories from a young age, it was only logical that the next step would be to write her own romances. She writes a cross section of everything genre. She recently started writing rural romance reflecting her long years of country living in regional Australia.

Fiona is a hybrid author with several independently published works and contracts with Escape Publishing and Tule Publishing.

Twitter & Instagram: @fionammarsden

Facebook Author Page:

https://www.facebook.com/PrincessFionaMarsden

Web: www.fionamarsden.com

Chelsea Locke

I adore Georgette Heyer's novel The Black Sheep and the romance between Abbie and Miles. It's where I first read the quote "Cabined Cribbed Confined" and loved it. So I wrote a story for Alicia and Rochford. They were surprised by their unexpected attraction when they first met in Berkeley Square.

Thanks to the Historical Loop on RWA Facebook, who answered my questions. Also to Debbie Deasey, who read my story, made terrific suggestions, and provided the story title. I love alliteration; Debbie triumphed with "Miss Marchant's Merriment".

I'm always up for a chat, so reach out:

Insta: chelsea_locke_romance_scribe_

Nicki Burns

Nicki Burns lives in regional New South Wales, a public servant by day and a writer by night, dreaming of love and romance under an enormous blue sky and a blistering sun. She writes slow-burn, high-heat RuRo novels.

You can find her on Twitter and Instagram, talking about writing, books, movies, politics, dogs and — mostly — food!

She believes that enemies to lovers, forced proximity and 'there's only one bed' are the best romance tropes.

Her dream is to one day see her book on the shelves at Big W.

Clare Miles

Clare Miles can't remember a time when she didn't love reading, and growing up in a big loud family it was the perfect escape. Years later her household isn't quite as noisy, but her love of reading and escape has never diminished, nor the desire to write her very own happily ever afters. She's absolutely thrilled to be part of the Sweet Treats Anthology for the second year in a row. She hopes you enjoys Sam and Josie's story as much as she did writing it!

You can find her at www.claremiles.com, on Instagram as Clare Miles Author, at www.facebook.com/clare.miles.7106, or in her favourite chocolate shop! "

Victoria Brown

Victoria Brown never imagined becoming a writer. Though she admits to penning the odd poem. The idea for a story sparked from a failed attempt at relaxation in a gonging tent. Busy with an accounting practice and family at the time, she tried to shove it aside. Only, it had other ideas.

When she retired, over a decade of dog-eared jottings evolved into her first manuscript. She hasn't stopped writing since and loves it.

Australia's beautiful countryside inspires her and often her characters. Women's challenges are her focus — with romance added of course.

She's on Facebook as <u>Victoria Brown Writes</u>.

Lucy Lever

Lucy Lever is a former social worker who lives in the bush on Sydney's coastal fringe with her husband.

Always an avid reader who would never think of going anywhere without a book, she decided to give creative writing a go late in life. Luckily it wasn't *too* late.

Lucy makes frequent visits to family on the NSW north coast, where she found the inspiration for her first novel, a rural rom com set in an alternative community to be published by Harlequin in September 2023.

Read more at Lucylever.com or follow Lucy on Instagram @lucy.lever.writer.

Caroline Deness

Caroline loves reading romance, humour and happy endings — doesn't everyone? She started writing when she ran out of books by her then favourite author, Janet Evanovich.

After all, there are only so many times a year a person can reread Georgette Heyer or Jane Austen, right?

Even more perfect was when Caroline discovered modern Regency Romance. She has a story in the RWAus 2019 Little Gems, *Tiger's Eye,* and 2021 Sweet Treats, *Chocolate,* anthologies. A big thank you to her 'avid readers of the genre'.

Find her at carolinedeness.com

Valerie G Miller

Valerie is a teacher and an author. Originally from Sydney, she now lives in Brisbane, Australia with her husband and daughter. Valerie completed a Master of Letters in Creative Writing in 2021. She has published an anthology of short stories and her first novel will be launched in 2022. Valerie is also working on a contemporary romance series. Her dog Mischa and cats, Daisy and Miss Lilly, are her writing companions. You will always find a novel and notebook filled with ideas and observations, tucked away in her handbag.

You can connect with Valerie via her website:

https://www.valeriegmiller.com

Or hang out with her socially on

Instagram @valerieg.miller

Facebook @valeriegmillerwriter

Kaaren Sutcliffe

Kaaren lives in Dalmeny on the South Coast of NSW. She is a previously published novelist, and a professional editor accredited with the Institute of Professional Editors. A freelance editor, she recently returned to writing and is working on a fantasy with romantic elements trilogy. *The Bridge* was inspired by her love of Japan and the beauty of the Dalmeny inlet. She has a B.A in Asian Studies with Honours in Japanese language, and in 2009 visited Ise and met two Ama divers as part of a guided tour. The story might well expand into a novel.

Annette Leigh

I live in Queensland but have spent much of my life in North Queensland. For the last three years I have been a full-time writer of 'Destination Mysteries with a Touch of Romance.'

I have written two unpublished novels — one set in Havana, Cuba, the second set in tropical North Queensland.

Apart from writing, I love to travel even though I've been limited to Queensland for the last couple of years.

The people I've met, places I've been, and the tricky situations in which I've found myself, have all provided inspiration for my stories and my characters.

Jillian Jones

Jillian Jones loves to explore the magical healing power of love in the contemporary romance genre. She also loves walking along the beach, her incredibly supportive husband and being entertained by two dramatic teenagers and two curious cats.

Her short stories have featured in the RWA anthology, 2016, 2017 and 2018 editions. And she's indie published a novella and two novels.

You can find more info at: www.jillianjones.com

Denise Aston

Denise Aston is the author of the Devils Warlords motorcycle club romance series where the sassy, strong-willed women and their sexy, alpha men work through their issues to get their own happily ever after.

Born in a small town in New Zealand, Denise grew up reading romance and dreaming of one day being able to write the stories that filled her head. Now, after adventuring overseas and working in corporate life for an eternity, her time has come and Denise is now back in rural New Zealand realising her dream of writing full time.

More at: www.deniseaston.com